THE WORLD'S OLDEST, MOST POWERFUL SECRET SOCIETY

THE WORLD'S OLDEST, MOST POWERFUL SECRET SOCIETY

By

Anand Arungundram Mohan

anandarungundrammohan@gmail.com

The World's Oldest, Most Powerful Secret Society
Anand Arungundram Mohan

www.2amcan-indian.com

All rights reserved
First Edition, 2019
© Anand Arungundram Mohan, 2019
Cover design © White Falcon Publishing, 2019

No part of this publication may be reproduced, or stored in a retrieval system, or transmitted in any form by means of electronic, mechanical, photocopying or otherwise, without prior written permission from the author.

Requests for permission should be addressed to anandarungundrammohan@gmail.com

ISBN - 978-1-9990906-1-6

Printed in Canada

Publisher's Cataloging-In-Publication Data
(Prepared by The Donohue Group, Inc.)

Names: Mohan, Anand Arungundram, author.
Title: The world's oldest, most powerful secret society / by Anand Arungundram Mohan.
Description: First edition. | [Vancouver, British Columbia] : 2Am Can-Indian Publisher, 2019. | Series: [The journey series] ; [1] | Interest age level: 010-018. | Summary: In the India of 261 B.C.E., King Ashoka the Great gathers together nine learned men to form a secret society and to write books on potentially destructive power which are then hidden. Later in present day Chennai, India, a group of children hear about this story and decide to search for the magic books in hopes of bringing their friend back to life.
Identifiers: ISBN 9781999090623 (hardcover) | ISBN 9781999090609 (paperback) | ISBN 9781999090616 (ebook)
Subjects: LCSH: Secret societies--India--Juvenile fiction. | Books--India--Juvenile fiction. | Children--Death--Juvenile fiction. | Voyages and travels--Juvenile fiction. | CYAC: Secret societies--India--Fiction. | Books--India--Fiction. | Death--Fiction. | Voyages and travels--Fiction. | LCGFT: Fantasy fiction.
Classification: LCC PZ7.1.M6382 Wo 2019 (print) | LCC PZ7.1.M6382 (ebook) | DDC [Fic]--dc23

Dedicated to my parents,

Shri. A.S. Mohan and Smt. Visalam Mohan

Previous book published:

The Under-Ordinary Life of Mangamma Uppertoe

Celebrities have extraordinary lifestyles, privileged with people at their beck and call, while the rest of us enjoy more peaceful and normal lives. Yet, among us "normal folk" are hundreds of thousands of people less fortunate who struggle just to make ends meet.

These underprivileged and unrecognized souls are slaves to poverty and an unforgiving environment, their struggles absent from our thoughts as we almost unconsciously try to avoid them, whether they are on the streets or toiling among us as day-to-day wage earners.

Abducted by fate, plagued by illusions, ravaged by the law and shunned by society, this significant part of our society has no hope of escape—except, maybe, for the very strongest and bravest. Follow the lives of three women who break all stigma and forge ahead without once retreating into the abyss they face.

The greatest fight is the conflict within oneself, especially when there is a reason to battle on. Brace yourself for the ultimate showdown and take heart from these women as they defend their freedom from all odds.

Table of Contents

Battle for non-violence 1

The Interaction 12

The Rescue Operation 18

The Incident.. 47

Parents' Constant Worries 88

The Mistake.. 92

The Book of Power.. 103

The Secret of the Swollen Girl.. 113

The Last Hurrah 139

Battle for non-violence

The year was 261 BC, and the war had just begun.

"We have lost our pride, my lord," the minister announced with concern.

"No need to doubt." King Ashoka was the embodiment of confidence. "We will regain Kalinga. The war may be short because our strengths are tremendous, and such a small kingdom will not overcome us. I have sent the best generals to oversee the battle—they are the most experienced and have worked under my father during his reign. I have complete faith they will achieve what they should in the earliest time possible."

"They were a part of our empire…," the minister seethed, "…but somehow, they got their independence. Our enemies might think we are puppies running after our tails for letting this happen. The trio-kingdoms in the southernmost part of this subcontinent have already defied us, even though they are small."

The minister could not keep his mouth shut for some time and was getting on Ashoka's nerves. They ended the discussion, and Ashoka retired to his chambers.

It was dark outside, and the birds were resting in the trees in his garden. The evening was quiet, and Ashoka gave a command to the soldier outside his bedroom. "Any time a report from the battlefield comes, please wake me up and do not bother waiting. I need a daily update. Make sure I get it, understood?"

Meanwhile, on the battlefield, the pep talk was going on.

The man had a crease on his forehead, deep lines like the Grand Canyon. He chewed on his mustache—a force of habit—and looked like a masked avenger with his white beard flowing down as smoothly as butter on a hot sunny day. He was a hefty man, strong enough to lift a pig, and sat atop a beautiful white horse with sparkling eyes. Turning his attention away from the enemy for a few minutes, he gave his final speech to the warriors about to take the field. In the darkness, the army had assembled.

The red ants would have been proud. The disciplined men were in sync with each other and moved as one. Youth was on their side, and with a brutal mindset, they were a perfect killing machine.

The oldest of them would have been thirty-five years of age. Six-pack abs were a common sight. The women would have drooled over them. The glint in their eyes was a shadow of the wrath they were about to unleash.

Not the best strategy to fight in the cloak of night, but it offered the opportunity of a surprise attack against the opposing army. The win could gain them the upper hand at the start of the war.

"*Beloved of the Gods* wants to us to reclaim what was ours. Be privileged to be part of this glorious opportunity, to serve your king and your country. Ask not what the nation has done for you. Ponder on what you can do for your nation. You will realize that you have been waiting for this all your life." His voice was soft and clear. However, the last man on the line could hear it. The silence of the dark was ominous.

There was pin-drop silence as he spoke, save for the occasional neighing of his horse and the other warhorses present.

None of the cavalrymen moved forward, lest they break the silence. It was the foot soldiers who marched in front of the cavalry.

The men didn't make a sound. They crept forward, hiding in the blanket of darkness as they marched over the distance separating them from the opponent's vast army stretched across the banks of the river Daya. If Kalinga's battalion was the size of a baseball, Ashoka's troops were the size of a baseball stadium. The determined men planned to take over Kalinga with no bloodshed.

"I will not ask you to always love me, God," a soldier with short, spring-like hair and a body to match his heart-shaped face mumbled to himself. "I will beg you to understand that what I am doing tonight is for duty and not for sport. Please forgive me for taking the lives of your children."

"Be quiet," warned his comrade-in-arms. A clean-shaven man, giant-sized and with a squinty eye, got irritated with this mushy talk.

It was then the captain gave a blood-curdling cry and set the ambush in motion. The rest of the troops followed, throwing fireballs into the enemy tents, which burned the men inside alive.

Drums sounded, background music to the grim happenings unfolding. The troops could not decipher if the sound was their thudding hearts or from hands pounding the cow skin spread across the drums.

The boom was fast-paced and urged the soldiers along on their mission, reminding them of the importance of their actions.

The fight was fierce. The smell of flesh burning joined the fragrance of the midnight sky. Sweat poured down their faces; each Kalinga warrior tried to make the best of the situation.

The clash of swords and the scramble to regain their footing caused confusion and chaos among Kalinga's officers. Ashoka's cavalry entered the scene, and the horses trampled over Kalinga's pajama-clad men.

What a joke, thought one giant soldier with a hairless face. Sleeping in tattered clothes—these soldiers are ill-equipped! A beggar has a better chance of fighting off the opponent.

The anticipation of an early victory vanished as Emperor Ashoka's men realized the tables had quickly turned.

Kalinga's men had rallied together under their captain. The strategy was to spread the enemy thin. The scattered men of Ashoka set many tents on fire, but were falling one by one like ripe mangoes falling on the ground.

That night—or, you could say, early morning—the captain dished out punishment to the watchers in the Kalinga battalion. He did not hang them—even though that was the popular vote from the army soldiers, who had come close to losing their lives.

The fight kept on for hours. They had designed the attack to penetrate the camp, reach Kalinga's general, and eliminate him.

"You watchers have not done your duty," cried the angry captain. Up and down, the furious man paced. How could he account for the loss and report this to his superiors? His bushy ears shivered. The anger in his voice was well-complemented by his blazing, brown eyes.

There was a huge cry from the gathered soldiers. "You allowed the foe to come and attack without giving us a warning. You will not die today because we need all the men to charge at the vast army in front of us. Tomorrow, you will head the charge. The tip of the spear, if you will, and you better be sharp."

Groans from the soldiers were the response to this

announcement, but discipline made them keep their calm and not cause a riot.

"In a few hours, the dawn will break, and the real fight will begin. The previous night's charge has served its purpose for them. We stayed up through the night. We are tired and too disoriented to put up a strong offense. So, the soldiers from the deeper parts of the camp who had enough rest in the night will take up their post while you take rest and recoup until you can give your best on the battlefield. Your orders are to kill at least three of the enemy's men before you succumb to your own wounds. Otherwise, I will haunt you in the afterlife."

"That is encouraging," one of the soldiers remarked under his breath, but no one around him paid any heed to this comment.

"Ashoka thinks he can conquer Kalinga, but we must respond the same way we responded to his grandfather, Chandragupta Maurya. We defended ourselves then, and we can do the same again. Go one step further and annex any land of Ashoka we can."

"Hear, hear," cried the soldiers.

"Let us squash them like grasshoppers," yelled a soldier, a call that was echoed throughout the crowd of armed men. It was so loud that Ashoka's men heard it, and it angered them.

At the break of dawn, both armies assembled on the field. The head of both armies approached. If this had been a movie scene, an energetic tune would have surely played in the background as they faced each other.

"Dogs!" cried Ashoka's men as they peered at the canines just ahead of Kalinga's army. It worried some. Fear of hounds was not uncommon, even among the strongest of men.

The snarling dogs had a rabid look in their red eyes, saliva drooling down from the sides of their mouths. Their tongues hung out, swaying like apes hanging from trees.

Feroz, one cavalryman, said, "Fear makes a man courageous when he overcomes it." The comment helped calm the men.

Feroz considered himself a philosopher. He had gotten angry when the people, impressed by his words, had recently called him a religious head. He had replied, "I am spiritual and not bound by any particular religion."

Sizing each other up, the two opposing generals met in the center.

"Give up now and surrender to King Ashoka." The general had a gleaming sword sheathed. Everyone knew it was more for show than use. In its heyday, the sword had dripped the blood of many an opponent.

"Never." The old man representing Kalinga knew of the impossible mission he had to accomplish. Fear was not present in his eyes. A defiance stronger than any armor adorned his face.

"Then we have nothing to talk about," the general with a double chin remarked. King Ashoka treated his men with abundance. Women, food, and riches were plentiful from all their conquests.

"Get out of Kalinga." In contrast, Kalinga's general looked like a starved tiger waiting to pounce on its prey. That made him dangerous. A slit for a nose, just enough to breathe the required amount of air for survival, seemed to expand in excitement.

"Like hell." His massive hands were balled into fists. Blood was not flowing properly. A yoga master would have said, Take a deep breath.

When Ashoka's general returned to his men, the captain remarked, "That was short."

"They need a lesson in humility. Destroy them right away," ordered the general.

They used the conch shell to blow a challenging cry for war. Kalinga's army unleashed the dogs and took to the skies in vimanas.

The vimanas were not unlike the chariots in *Ben Hur*. Only these were different in that they could fly. An anti-gravity vehicle for stealth and efficiency. A deadly tool that couldn't be brought down by ordinary arrows.

No need to fret if the wheels were punctured. They didn't need to run on ground, anyway.

Many of the dogs were killed by the arrows that flew across the battlefield, but some vicious canines survived and pounced on the soldiers.

With shields, the soldiers defended themselves while charging at the same time. They used swords to slaughter the rabid creatures.

The two armies clashed.

The ring of steel clashing was deafening. There were spears, as sharp as a pencil used for an exam. It kept the fiercest of warriors from crossing it. When men face adversity such as this, the results can be extraordinary—*Ripley's Believe it or Not* could have taken shot after shot of what occurred that day in history.

Feroz jumped over the barricade erected and killed a dozen soldiers before his horse got its head chopped off and got thrown to the ground.

He sliced and diced his way through his enemies. They

cornered him in three directions, but he warded off the weapons with fast countermoves.

With well-coordinated strokes and arms moving in a smooth river-like flow, he brought death to his foes. His black beard swished and swayed with the wind as he danced around with his weapon.

"Take that, you mongrels," he screamed as he beheaded opponents one by one. In a heart-stopping moment, a blood-soaked sword cut his shoulder blade through the armor, injuring him a bit. Not a serious wound in this battleground. There were people with dislocated arms swiping at the enemy with their still-attached hand.

Hours passed, and both sides were feeling the pinch. In the evening, the men returned to their respective camps, tired and worn out but still on constant lookout for any last-minute surprises.

Feroz was one survivor of the bloody war, and he got no rest that night. He was sent as a messenger back to Ashoka to report on the day's events.

Ashoka was waiting. The marble floor in his bedroom gleamed against the night sky. The fireplace's light reflected off the surface, making shadows dance. However, in contrast, the king was steady and immobile, like a blot of ink on a piece of parchment.

"What took you so long?" the emperor asked with annoyance.

"Sorry, my lord," Feroz replied, giving no explanation. He knew better than to contradict his head of state.

"Tell me, what word from the battlefield?"

"Our generals waged the war with wisdom. That is the reason we lost less than those of our enemy." Feroz took a breath before continuing. "We had lodged a preemptive attack last night, and it was a success. Your army killed many people."

That was the last sentence he would ever speak. A sword pierced his heart the very next day. His spouse and two children received the news that evening. They were proud of his sacrifice.

The frontline fought with courage. Some days Ashoka knew they were on the winning side, but some days he felt lost. When Ashoka won, there was no man left in the Kingdom of Kalinga.

Every able-bodied man from Kalinga had picked up a sword and waged an all-out war. They preferred to die on their feet rather than live on their knees.

The total number of soldiers who died numbered a quarter million, and both sides lost an equal number of troops.

The brute strength of Ashoka's army had brought them victory. However, something happened that day—an event that made historians remember this as the bloodiest battle with a twist in the end.

"We will never engage in war again," said Ashoka after surveying the battlefield. "I am so shameful that I caused so many deaths. From now on, I will follow the path of ahimsa—or non-violence," he vouched.

Historians wrote this to be the first and only instance in which the victor chose to lay down arms for good. That was when he became known as: "Ashoka, the Great."

In the decade following the war, there was peace and harmony throughout the kingdom. King Ashoka the Great founded a secret society comprised of nine brilliant men.

"You will all search for information in different fields. Please begin with psychological warfare. If there is a fight yielding results without the loss of a single life, then I wish to know how to do that." The king drew a calming breath. "Another field I am interested in is not a new one. I want to know about physiology and figure out the touch of death," he explained to the nine men.

The other topics covered by the emperor were:

1. Microbiology

2. Alchemy

3. Communication with alien life

4. Anti-gravity and Indian UFOs

5. Time travel

6. Changing the speed of light

"There is only one condition," continued the king. "This must remain a secret. About 10,000 years ago, there was a kingdom in which the ruler was a god named Rama. His kingdom got destroyed by Atlantis, which was, in retaliation, destroyed by him. During that era, there have been many technological advances that need recording for the benefit of humanity. That is your sacred and secret duty.

"We will work for the good of the world and reveal ourselves to those who are worthy. In a time of dire need, we take control to bring harmony. We shall work to gather knowledge. To hide this critical information from the rest of the world is our main priority. It will not fall into the hands of evildoers."

With the king's words in mind, these nine men searched and researched for all the relevant data. They used this information to better humanity and to shape the destiny of the world.

They kept their promise and hid these books of power.

A secret society would normally meet in an underground setting with lamps cradling the walls. But you must remember: This was the first of the secret societies and had a lot to learn.

In the middle of the king's private garden, the nine men met. Wearing robes that flowed in the wind, the tall men smiled.

One of the nine men was Raza. He was a sharp man with skin stretched tight over his muscles. There was not an extra pound on him. His hooked nose and V-shaped chin made him look like a hawk.

"Raza, you take my book of anti-gravity, and I will take your book of communications to protect it."

The man who said this could not have been more in contrast to Raza. He was portly with a broad nose on a round, pudgy face.

All nine men disappeared in different directions to search for a place to hide the books. Raza set out from present-day Odisha in search of the right place to bury the book.

The Interaction

One day, while Raza was whistling to himself and walking in the woods under the shady trees and the cool breeze, he found himself face to face with a lion.

To the untrained ear, the lion growled. But Raza was a communications expert and could understand what the lion said.

Like a person wearing slippers with no need to carpet the floor of the Earth to protect from a thorn, Raza had all languages translated before it reached his ears. Like a google translator, but a more efficient one.

It worked both ways; his words got converted to whatever language he wanted. Whether it be man or beast, it meant anyone could understand and talk to him.

"Leave me be," Raza replied. As far as the lion knew, Raza was growling too. "I mean you no harm. I demand to go on my way."

"Go your way?" the lion roared, incredulous at the very thought. "I don't think so. I am famished. You will make an excellent meal for me. Are you ready to meet your maker?" The lion paused for a second, considering what Raza had said. "This is nothing personal, just business. Perhaps there are other ways to fill my belly, but I will not eat vegetables. You understand me?"

Realizing the lion couldn't be reasoned with, Raza turned on his heel and ran as fast as his trembling legs would carry him.

"There is no point," the lion teased as it gave chase. "You are just wasting your energy. Give up now, and it will be painless. Do you think I cannot catch up to you? I may be old, but I am not out."

Near a cliff overlooking the river, the beast cornered Raza.

"I am on an important mission," Raza cried, desperate to get away. "Why don't you understand that? There is no time to waste. I must be on my way."

"Meal on heels," the lion purred, licking its chops. "You cannot escape me. I cannot, at this age, run and catch a deer. If I could do that, I wouldn't be bothering you, now would I? However, you have aroused my curiosity, and I would like to learn about your mission."

Raza grabbed onto the opportunity to keep the lion occupied and told the beast of his quest.

The lion considered. "Too bad you are going to be eaten. Or I would recommend you go to a city called Madras. It is outside the border of your kingdom, and no one would ever suspect you have hidden anything there."

Raza jumped from the cliff and hoped to God that he would not land on the rocks.

He did not drown that day, even though he was not a good swimmer. The river was deep enough to soften his landing. He gasped for oxygen while flailing and bobbing up and down in the water.

"Over here! That crazy man jumped all the way from up there," shouted someone from the riverbanks.

Raza turned to see an old man with more wrinkles on his face than *Cruella de Vil* had spots on her dalmation coat. He had a cloth covering his ears.

Another man who seemed much younger accompanied him, but his eyes were covered in fabric.

Between them, helping Raza was a backbreaking and time-consuming process. Once back on his feet, Raza leaned on the nearby rocks in exhaustion.

"Give him some space," ordered the elderly sage. The younger gentleman moved away, and the pair waited for Raza to finish spouting out water. "Th-thank you," he at last muttered.

"No problem! What are you doing?" the aged man croaked. His voice sounded as weak as he was.

Raza was searching his backpack, which was a water-resistant one. He gave a sigh of relief when he saw that the book was in good condition.

"My name is Raza. I meant to travel by foot to Madras. Can you aid me, please?"

"Why did you jump? That was such a foolish move." The old man had not introduced himself but was pounding Raza with questions.

"I had no choice. A lion attacked me, and so I jumped. I had been trapped, and I had nowhere else to go." Raza was shaking like a kettle on a burning stove.

"You are cold, coming out of the river," the old man observed. "We can get acquainted over a hot cup of tea."

The three walked down a winding forest path. Raza was dripping water, and the wind seemed to pierce his bones. His rescuers did not appear to have any dry towels to help him, and he wanted to reach the cottage as soon as possible.

After a quick five-minute walk, they reached their destination. The little hut felt cozy. It was a home filled with compassion and kindness. The floor was made of mud and clay. It was washed daily with freshly acquired cow dung.

Raza dried himself off and thanked them for the hot cup of tea. He looked through the window to analyze his surroundings. The trees blocked his view. The entire place was nestled between thick-barked trees. A small clearing in the middle for prayer was man-made.

Raza knew the night was going to be as dark as the Mariana Trench.

"My name is Kasi, and I am blind," the younger man said. "That is why I am wearing a kerchief over my eyes." He gestured to his older companion. "And this is my Guruji, Jaganath, and he cannot hear."

Sitting cross-legged on the dung-covered ground, Raza gazed around the small living room. It was a clean place with everything in order. A stool stood next to the window.

Other than that, there were few furnishings in the place. It was a simple dwelling, with a painting of a goddess hanging on the wall.

The paint on the inside was a shade of sky-blue that made the home's inhabitants instantly feel comfortable. It was a good contrast to the outside greenery.

"Hence, he is wearing a cloth over his ears," finished Raza.

"That is correct," Kasi agreed, shaking his head. "There are six of us living here. Each with a disability, such as lacking the ability to taste, touch, et cetera."

Raza wanted to leave, but his whole body was aching.

"You can stay here for the night," Jaganath said with kindness. The bed was comfortable, and Raza was tired. He nodded off as soon as his head hit the pillow.

He curled up like a baby. The moonlight gently caressed his face, and the wind rocked the branches nearby.

The silence was a blanket in itself. The amount of carbon dioxide absorbed by the trees was abundant. Raza breathed in the unhealthy night air. His sleep was still deep from all the running he had done.

Sprinting from the lion had taken a toll on him. His tired eyelids did not open till sunrise.

The next morning, Raza woke up still wishing he had more time to rest. He was on a mission and could not waste precious time.

"I have not seen the others. I wish I could have met them before leaving." Raza spoke to Kasi. Kasi made a gesture that his guru understood. *A type of sign language? Neat*, thought Raza. It intrigued him. He knew he had to come up with a spell to overcome this particular barrier. A true communication expert's passion came alive.

"They have gone to the nearby village to get supplies. They will be back tomorrow or the day after that."

"How can I ever repay you?" Raza asked.

"If you wish to compensate me, then there is a way. In the valley below, there is a boy named Gautham. Every day he toils in the fields, and every night he gets beaten up by his drunken stepfather. I have sometimes been unfortunate enough to listen to his cries in the evening. Everyone knows about him. Can you help him?"

It outraged Raza to hear this. How could anyone be so cruel? Alcohol could bring out the worst in people. He promised to take the boy and care for him.

Before leaving, Raza checked his belongings and even opened the secret book of power to read it and confirm that there was nothing missing. He felt ashamed to suspect his saviors, but there was something huge at stake, and he could not risk it at any cost.

The book was brown and bound in wood—not leather or paper, but actual wood. All the nine books looked alike. This one had a seal in the middle: a power sign.

It was surprisingly light for such a thick book. That was the only difference among the nine books. The length of each book varied significantly, depending on the amount of information available.

The Rescue Operation

Raza kept walking toward the valley and got there in about fifty minutes time. It was a brisk walk, and the morning air was refreshing.

He spied a small boy—just a teenager—toiling in the nearby fields. He was chocolate-brown but had several whip marks across his back. The sight saddened Raza. He wanted to help this lad, who had been exposed to a lot of hardships, despite his youth.

Raza had waited for hours until the sun set behind the mountains. It was a breathtaking sight, colors painting the sky with orange light like a canvas drawn with the divine hand.

"Just a little more time," Raza said to himself. He sat down on the ground and fiddled with the twigs that had fallen from a nearby tree.

At last, the stars came out, and the drunkard walked into the clearing. The stepfather had been loitering around the girls' hostel. When he was finally shooed away, he had gone to the local watering hole.

He had made a scene there and got kicked out. He was in a foul mood, with more liquor in him than a sultan's brewery.

He held the boy by his hair, and the man screamed vulgar words. Raza had to hold himself back. He knew that it would spoil the plan if he acted right now. It would serve the purpose for a short while, but in the long run it would not make any sense.

The drama continued for an hour, and the villagers did not seem to care, as it was a routine practice.

"What is my name, boy?" the man demanded.

"Sredharan, sir."

"And do I look like a fool to you?"

"Not particularly."

"Who drank all my beer, dear boy?"

"You drank it all." The defiance of this bony, roughed-up teen enthralled Raza.

"Liar." And with that final word the stepfather took out his belt and whipped the little boy left, right, and center. The boy did not even try to defend himself. He had given up on all hope of salvation.

Later, Raza saw that Sredharan had gone off to sleep, and the boy was cleaning up the empty bottles. Raza made his way forward and hid behind a tree. He called the boy's name.

"Gautham, Gautham," Raza whispered.

Gautham thought he was dreaming. Who would call at this unearthly hour? He turned and saw a figure next to the tree. Clad all in black and standing against the night, the man seemed to be invisible.

"Can I help you?" Gautham asked, and the pain of the recent beating echoed in his voice.

"It is I who needs to help you. You carry so many burdens. I don't know what to say or how to say it, but I was wondering if you would like to have a life without being beaten up every day. Think of me as a traveler going to Madras. If you want to come with me, I will care for you and give you your freedom from this violent life."

There was a pin-drop silence. "You're not joking?" the boy whispered back. It all seemed too remarkably good to be true, and he knew that if something was too perfect to be true, then it was not.

"Far from it," Raza replied. "I'm as serious as can be, and I would appreciate your company."

The boy broke into a smile, an expression that hid his pain and showed how jubilant he was at the thought of escape. His sparkling white teeth could have lit the way forward.

"What do you want me to do? Do I need to pack anything?" Then the boy answered his own question by adding, "I need to pack some food...clothing?"

"Don't worry about all that. Just come with me. I will help you like the way the Saints helped me. I will buy you clothes, and I have food to share, so don't worry about it," he reassured the boy.

Raza and his young new companion walked away from the hut. After a few steps, the boy turned and rushed back, and the sudden turn of events shook Raza. He followed the boy and tried to not wake anyone up.

He saw that there was a horse tied nearby. Gautham had rushed to the animal and was untying it.

"I do not want to leave my horse behind," Gautham explained. "It could be useful for us if you have come by foot. If we ride him, it will save us time. Neither of us are heavy, and so we can both ride without a problem."

"Good thinking," said Raza.

Both got away from the boy's old home as speedily as possible, and the clippity-clop of the horse's hooves were the only sounds throughout their entire journey. At dawn, they both lay down to rest in the fields. They had tired the horse as well, and it dozed off standing nearby. They slept for four hours, even though the sun was blazing. Soon after, they woke up and walked toward the horizon. The horse was not pleased to be roused from its slumber, but it obliged to the commands of his master.

At around noon, the boy's father, Sredharan, woke up with a severe headache. The hangover did not leave him in good spirits.

"Gautham," he called expectantly, but no one responded. He waited for two minutes and then yelled, "Where in blazes are you, boy? Bring me some spring water. My arms are sore from hitting you all night. You need to boil oil for my bath."

A wall had a better probability of answering him. Finally, he slouched forward and, taking one step at a time, edged toward the door. The sun shone, and Sredharan blinked. Squinting, he sensed the boy was nowhere close to the fields.

He wondered where his son could have gone. This was unusual. *He needs punishment*, thought Sredharan.

He waited till lunchtime, but the boy didn't return. That is when Sredharan knew something fishy was going on, and he needed to find out what. He was a master huntsman and could track all kinds of beasts.

There were footprints alien to his house. *Someone has been here,* he realized.

He soon found out the horse was missing; so, he ran to see in which direction they had ridden.

The hungover stepfather packed food and followed the tracks of the horse. He traveled mostly during the day and rested only late in the night.

He had made good time and knew that he was not particularly far away from getting his hands on that cursed boy. That evening, Sredharan did not drink. All he wanted to do was cause violence.

He slept for five hours, got up before sunrise, and was soon well on his way.

"These guys are slow," he mused and laughed to himself devilishly. He passed through the meadows, the fields, and across the rivers until he reached the city that afternoon.

The city that never slept invited the fiend in. The cobbled roads with streetlamps loomed overhead like overarching branches of a willow tree.

The bustling crowd paid no attention to the traveler with his own agenda.

Lucky for him—but not so much for Gautham—he found where they were staying. It was a rickety old place. A dimly lit, perfect-for-hiding establishment.

The building was in a cul-de-sac. Unless a guy was an expert at following trails, this was an improbable place to find.

"Hey, I know you're in there. Come out and play," Sredharan yelled. The passersby stopped to see what the commotion was.

Raza came out of the inn and said, "Get out of here." Gautham was peeping out of the second-floor window. A tiny crack in the curtain was all anyone could see from outside.

"This man kidnapped my son, my only child. I have lost my wife, and he is the only family I have. I don't know what he thinks about himself, but he kidnapped my son," Sredharan lamented out loud to the gathered crowd.

The public turned their gaze toward Raza and wondered what he had to say in his defense. But before Raza could open his mouth, a small voice shouted across the still evening air.

"Liar, liar, your pants are on freaking fire. You do not treat me well, and you expect me to come back to you. I don't think so." With that said, Gautham removed his shirt and showed the marks on his skin: the cruelty of his stepfather.

"Don't you dare talk that way. I know that sparing the rod only leads to a child being spoiled. You will know something about parenting only when you become a father yourself. This is not the way to talk to an elder. You remember that," warned Sredharan.

"The bottom line is that Gautham does not want to come with you, so leave him be," Raza interjected. "I would take care of him, and I will let no harm come to him if it is the last thing I ever do. Even if that harm comes from you."

"How dare you accuse me that way? Draw your weapon," Sredharan said and lashed out with an ax he had brought along, intending to chop off the head of the person who stole his child.

Raza had no weapon on him, and seeing the other man raise a weapon startled him. He came back to reality, knowing that this might be the last day of his life. That gave him the courage to resist like a madman. Knowing he was fighting for a just cause made him a dangerous man to cross.

The crowd scattered away, leaving the two men to their fate. They did not want to witness a murder.

Sredharan swung his ax and cut Raza near his chest, who backed away until he hit a stone wall. He thought to himself, *How many times am I going to let somebody corner me?* He hated the situation he now found himself in.

Before Sredharan could swing his ax again, Raza punched his opponent in the nose. Sredharan swore out loud as blood poured from his nostrils.

Raza dove for cover and landed next to a pigsty. He was breathing hard, his gut aching as his stamina gave out. Sredharan laughed, advancing on Raza. He was savoring the moment he had been waiting for.

With no one around to help, Raza felt sheer desperation. It was in that instant that Gautham showed his loyalty to Raza by jumping on Sredharan and distracting him.

Sredharan kicked Gautham in the stomach and sent him reeling. That angered Raza, and he did what he could do well. He spoke with the pigs that were there, asking them for help, and help they did, charging at Sredharan. Their aggression was turbulent. Sredharan threw the ax, and it landed in Raza's thigh.

Raza screamed; the pain in his leg was beyond measure. Gautham rushed to him with the horse and helped him get on top. Gautham gave one last scornful look at Sredharan before getting on the horse; they both galloped away at high speed.

They reached the outskirts of the city fast, but it was all barren land from there on out.

"What I am about to do might scare you, but do not worry. I am there for you," Raza spoke with a tenderness that shook the boy to the bones.

This made Gautham curious. Raza opened the book of power and chanted a few lines. Before they knew it, the horse rose from the ground and flew. The anti-gravity spell had worked.

"I needed to use this to get through our neighbor's border, anyway. The unconquered southern part of our peninsula is where we are heading," Raza explained.

Raza was in immediate need of a doctor; he was losing blood. The horse galloped in the skies without being noticed and without a sound. The fresh air made Gautham feel alive, but he was concerned about Raza's wound.

Raza was slipping in and out of consciousness. He left it to the boy to figure out where they were heading.

Gautham's hand was shivering, and it was not from the chill air. He had an idea of where they were going.

Every now and then, Raza would whisper to the horse and make sure they were making good progress.

But Gautham was gripping the reins with bloodless hands. He was worried he could make a mistake that would lead to the death of his rescuer. He would not let that happen.

A few teardrops trickled down his face. He might be too young to save Raza's life.

"Please don't go to sleep, and if you see a white light, for heaven's sake, stay away from it," Gautham whimpered.

It felt like they had traveled for hours, but finally they reached their destination, and Gautham directed the horse back toward Earth.

"Where can I find a doctor?" he asked a man standing on the road, but the man just stared at him without replying.

The road itself was crooked and dusty. It was broad enough for two modern-day trucks to go side by side.

People were clothed differently here. The boy had never seen the like. Dhotis and bare-chested men passed by, followed by women in saris.

None of them spoke the boy's language. Sign language came into the limelight again. Gautham tried to get the meaning across. *Are we not in the same kingdom?* the boy wondered. *How could they not speak Urdu?*

Gautham was panicking, but he heard Raza say, "This is a different part of the world.... They will not understand your language." Raza then spoke to the man and inquired about the whereabouts of a doctor.

Raza felt as weak as a newborn baby as they reached the doctor. Gautham helped him up and took him inside the house.

The house looked grand. It was indeed a wealthy man's home. Jewels decorated the walls. It was a safe place. No one thought to rob anyone in those days. It was a time of plenty.

After looking at Raza and taking care of his wounds, the doctor said, "Give it a week's rest, and then you can be on your way again—wherever you are going. We don't get that many visitors over here from other parts of the world, but it is Tamilian culture to welcome all guests to our homes. What I'm trying to say is that you are welcome to stay here and take rest for the following week, and then you can continue your journey."

Raza was amazed at the hospitality. A simple man in a rich mansion? He never dreamed of it. Such a welcoming heart. This man had indeed been blessed with good looks. Muscular and well-defined, his skin tone was dark-brown. A sturdy mouth and thick eyebrows made his features all the more appealing to the gentler gender.

Raza and Gautham took refuge there. The days had flown past. Their fatigue from their journey was replaced with the excitement of accomplishing Raza's goal. They made their way to Thiruvarur instead of Madras as the lion had suggested. They traveled light because they were close to the end. No need to weigh down the horse with extra luggage.

Raza did not want any creature to know where he was hiding the book, including the lion.

Heroes' and Heroines' Birth

On one particular day in the year 2006, nine kids were born. I'm sure that in the world over nine would have been born on one day, but for our story, we concentrate on the nine born in a building called "River Fall."

The building had ninety flats. It was raining cats and dogs on that day, making it hard for the fathers to visit the hospital, return home, and come back again.

Ram was the eldest of the nine children born by nine minutes. He was a cute little thing with arms and legs soft and cuddly. His mother could not hold back the tears of joy that rolled down her cheeks when she saw her baby for the first time.

Ten years down the line, the children grew fond of each other and always were in each other's company while playing cricket just outside River Fall. Of the nine that were born, seven were boys, and two were girls.

The girls were more interested in playing hide and seek, since they could hide for long periods of time, while the boys grew impatient and got caught quickly. The girls were also faster runners and could beat the boys in a hundred-meter dash.

When they finished their primary schooling at age twelve, they had their first excursion with their parents and friends. They visited water parks and theme parks and had a whale of a time.

Ram, the undoubted leader of the gang, knew how to swim. His father encouraged him to jump from a nine-foot diving board. Although Ram's limbs always shook before the jump, he would obey his dad. His father would be in the swimming pool waiting to help if Ram needed it.

The dark-skinned boy had just had a root canal done. *Too much chocolate,* the doctor had warned. Ram was skinny and lanky. He was a good sprinter and a strong short-put champion.

He was supposed to wear spectacles, but he was against it. His eyes weren't the right shape. There was no issue otherwise. "I am fine," he always insisted adamantly.

Leela, another of the nine children, loved to read books. She had dark hair that flowed down her shoulders and hips. She was constantly taking care of it—a labor of love.

Her skin was smooth, but she had a birthmark on her left shoulder. A mole of sorts. It was red and quite visible. She did not appreciate it being there and hid it well.

She was the one who coined the term "The Nifty Nine" after reading "The Secret Seven" and "The Famous Five" novels. They had a secret code to enter the room. No one was allowed to be part of their meetings without it.

The parents found these behaviors funny, but they did not discourage it.

"It's your birthday tomorrow. I mean, our birthday tomorrow. All of us. Shall we go out to someplace or have a party at home?" Leela was always excited about an outing.

The nine were sitting at a roundtable conference type of setting in Leela's house. Her parents were affluent and had an expert interior specialist work at making their home look luxurious.

There was an idol of Shiva as a centerpiece. He looked positively fearsome and grand.

The living room was spacious, with a neat wooden table and four chairs. As the children grew up in the same setting, the parents had decided to make the kid's room the biggest one. Most of the time, the children assembled there.

They even had their own makeshift table for their meetings.

"I think we should have a vote on this. Let's go by the majority and have fun either way. If it were me, I think I would like to go out to the beach and enjoy the waves. All those in favor of going out for our birthday, raise your hands." Ram was just as excited for a good time.

A general discussion ensued over what to do. After about five minutes, the entire team put their hands up and cried, "Let's go out."

So that decided that, and they notified the parents.

Rocky was the lovable type and the happiest of the lot. The girls thought that his smile could always lighten their mood. A bubbly, outgoing type, he was the heart of the group. He was always up for anything. He also had a few extra pounds on him.

The mothers of Ram and Rocky each took their car and drove the children to the beach.

"Don't go too deep into the water," they took turns warning. And they repeated "be careful of the current" over and over again.

The sandals came off Rocky's feet. The sand was hot, and

the wind was cool. A moment's breath to inhale the fresh sea breeze, and then he raced to the waters. He passed by a huge horse with a hefty man atop it. The man spat *paan*, a type of leafy after-lunch kind of mouth-freshener.

There was an old man selling balloons near a fat lady who spoke with a lisp who was selling toys. She had a variety of them. An Indian *Toy Story* movie would be fun to watch, what with the colorful skirts and shaking heads, those dolls would have made any child's heart ache.

The water was a little rough as it crashed on the shore, each wave more forceful than the previous one.

The adults themselves were wary of the water. They did not seem to go in too deep. The Bay or Bengal Ocean is not a body of water anyone would mess around with.

Do children know that? Of course not. Especially teens. Rocky was waist-deep in the water, and he dipped his head under the surface now and then.

"Come back, Rocky," Gopal warned, but Rocky did not pay him any attention. Gopal was the worrying type. He cared more for others than he did for himself. He went out of his way to help and assist the elderly.

He made sacrifices without saying a word. The girls loved his caring attitude. It melted their hearts. The boys, reluctant though they may be, also could not help but adore this young man with a big heart.

Carrying a few pounds on him, Gopal was not aiming to be the next Sylvester Stallone. You were not going to find him boxing Mike Tyson or playing a high-contact sport anytime soon. He was a careful and sensitive boy.

"What a beautiful moon," said Rocky's mother, and for a moment it distracted Rocky as he gazed at the heavens above. It was a full moon, causing a gravitational pull that made the tide rise. A massive wave hit Rocky square in the face and knocked him off balance.

The current pulled him into deeper waters. The children panicked and shrieked from the shore. They could see Rocky's head bobbing in and out of the water.

"I will go get him," said Ram, and before anyone could stop him, he jumped into the water and swam with powerful strokes. Renewed cries of dismay erupted from the shore.

"Is there a lifeguard over here? Is there anyone who knows how to swim in the ocean?" Ram's mother shrieked at the top of her lungs. She nearly felt her trachea blow up from the effort.

There were thirty-to-forty people crowded near the scene. No one replied, and there was complete silence except for the dancing waves.

Indians are not endowed with the strongest of bodies. Any human is weak against nature.

"Rocky, I'm coming to get you!" Ram yelled, proving that physical strength was nothing compared to the love of a friend. By this time, Rocky had no more energy, and he was drowning. To save him, Ram dove underwater.

The water was not clear, and he could not see far; there was debris all over. All the waste from the city seemed accumulated in this area. Ram cursed but continued to search for his friend.

A big fish swam by, and Ram hoped to God that it was not a shark. At long last, he found Rocky unconscious and floating toward the bottom of the sea. He plunged deeper and pulled Rocky to the surface. Rocky's head broke through, and he began coughing non-stop, but at least he had regained consciousness.

Ram and Rocky felt their arms lose their strength, but with the determination that only children can muster, they swam harder.

As they neared the shore, half the beach came to greet them. People were applauding the courage and friendship between these two boys.

There was commotion all over, but they gave the boys some room to recover while peppering them with questions.

"Are you all right?"

"Is there anything we can do for you?"

"Are you cold?"

The questions continued gushing in from all corners, but Ram had no intention of answering any of them.

After about ten minutes of coughing and spluttering out water, Rocky sat up. "I realized something," he told his mother and the others surrounding him. "The moon is round, bright, and beautiful tonight."

All the people smiled.

"Next time around, don't let the moon distract you. I told you not to go into the deep water, but you would not listen. This happens if you do not listen to your elders. We were once your age. You have nothing to prove, and no one to impress. Learn to be more careful," chided his mom.

"Shall we go on or shall we go home?"

"We can't let this small thing ruin our day. We have to carry on and enjoy as much as we can, because it's cool now. It's all cool now," Rocky said.

"So, what do you wish to do?" Leela piped up. "I want to go horse riding." She eyed the horse that was trotting nearby.

It was a common sight for the beach to be riddled with entertaining ponies. Children rode them and so did the fat adults. It was a costly affair, but a thrilling experience. The owners of the horse ran alongside for safety.

"That's a wonderful idea. I too want to go."

"Me too."

"Me three."

Everyone laughed. The mood lightened. The horse was dark-brown and had a patch of white stripes painted on its forehead.

A few more horses and their masters came to offer their services when they saw the number of children.

"I want peanuts...roasted. And *chollam*." Leela had been fascinated with those from the first time she had sunk her teeth into that delicious corn. She liked them with a bit of salt and *garam masala, a* powdered form of spices.

The nearby vendor, who sold peanuts, informed them that the price was Rs. 10 for a handful of peanuts. There were quite a few folk from the poorer section of the community selling anything and everything on the beach.

The children ate while they rode with the wind ruffling their hair. The trot soothed their mood. They moved as one with their beasts.

"This is the best birthday ever. Can you give me a few more coins?" Gopal was energized.

"Yes, we want to buy a kite," added Ali. Ali had a temper that would scare any adult. He had a nose like that of a sawfish. Pointy and long, it well-represented his sharp mind.

And buy a kite, they did. The man who sold it had grizzled hair that had not been washed in weeks. He had a variety of them.

The kite they purchased was a big, rectangular-shaped, long-tailed, red-colored one brightened further by a picture of a dragon. The kite caught their interest, and they took turns flying it.

"It is getting dark, we cannot see the kite anymore, and we can't fly it if we can't see it."

"That is true. What do you want to play?"

"Let us go someplace else."

"Where?"

Rocky looked up at the moon and said, "Why not the planetarium?" It was not too long a drive through the city. The roads had their bumps along the way.

It is terrifying to drive through these open manholes, thought Ram's mom. She evaded them as successfully as any other driver on the road.

"That is an excellent idea," said Ali.

The whole party drove to the nearby planetarium, famous for its exciting programs about stars.

It was a bit of a walk. There was a sense of calm and serenity attached to the institute. *When I grow up, I would like to go on the tracks,* thought Ali. There was a go-kart arena right there that triggered this idea. It was expensive for them, though.

They paid the entrance fee and got in. They shared all the expenses for that day between the families of the nine children. So, the funding was enough to cover all the costs incurred.

"Ice cream." Ali was drooling with anticipation. "I want ice cream."

"I want the chocolate flavor." Ram piped up.

"Vanilla flavor for me." Leela was happy. She gripped her cone a little too strongly and nearly crushed it in her hands.

"I will have butterscotch," Rocky said shyly. He was the one who took the shortest time to finish it.

And so the list extended. Sales that day were good for the ice cream vendor sitting outside the planetarium.

With the ice cream dripping all over, the reclining chairs made them look at the screen above.

"I feel sleepy. The room is dark, and the air-conditioner is on. What more do you need?" whispered Ali. The outside temperature was uncomfortably hot. The mothers were happy to rest a while.

Ram chuckled.

"Keep quiet. The program is about to begin, and I am interested to see what they have scheduled for today. I prefer to see planets that are much larger than Earth. I want to see how hot the sun is. I want to know if we are at the center of our galaxy. I want to feel—" Leela was descriptive to the playful annoyance of the other kids.

"We get the picture," Gopal said in an irritated fashion. He wanted to know when this program would be over so they could get out of there. Gopal wanted to go home and sleep.

He wanted to watch the latest *Swat Kats* episode before that. He loved those cartoons. He was a late bloomer who did not act like a teen.

The first of the stars peeped out from the screen placed above and around them. Silence set in. However, the theater was not "house full." Half the available seats were empty that day.

"We are born from the stars. Every atom in our body comes from gasses from the stars. Today, we will talk about what happens when the stars die. It is an interesting phenomenon, and they call it the black hole. The gravitational force is strong like a high tide during a full moon. Even light can get sucked in. No one knows what lies beyond that. We can only guess, and I suppose it is not enough to prove anything. Scientists all over the world are interested in this phenomenon...."

Gopal slipped off his chair, having already dozed off during the program. The person who was conducting it had a captivating voice, and it was lulling him to sleep.

With a huge thud, he landed on the ground. Everyone turned to look, concerned, and then laughter erupted from Ali, followed by everyone else in the party.

Gopal got up. Rubbing his back, he couldn't stifle his yawn. He was a little embarrassed, but he joined in the laughter too.

"You okay, there?" questioned Leela.

"Yeah, not bad." Gopal was red-faced like a blushing buffoon.

"You might not think any of this is interesting, but it is actually very informative and spectacular. I don't know why boys don't like to grow their stupid brains," Leela scolded.

"Don't be too harsh on him. The interest varies from one person to another, and what you might like may not be to the liking of another," Rocky said. He had enjoyed the show and felt disappointed that Gopal did not.

"You always come to his rescue. He is not a kid, you know. He's the same age as us."

"Some people take more time to mature than others," Rocky piped up.

The program master finished the show with, "...NGC 1277 is one of the biggest black holes known to us."

Leela turned to see if Gopal had dozed off again. She caught him looking at her. He immediately looked away. Leela smiled.

The gang filed out of the planetarium.

That night they slept well, as they were all tired. The next day was a school day.

Gopal woke up late and was close to missing the bus to school. He had put on his socks in such a hurry that he realized they were inside out when he reached his school.

School was as boring as usual, and the teachers kept droning about this and that. For the second time, Gopal fell asleep. Till the end of the class, no one disturbed them.

When the bell rang, Gopal got up. The class monitor moved to the front of the room and faced them. He was a boy short for his age who wore glasses. He seemed to take school a little too seriously.

"I have some rather important information to give you all. The cricket match that the Hyderabad school is hosting next month is something we would like to win. So, tryouts will be after school. If you are interested, you know where to be." The short boy with the glasses seemed bored to announce it. He did not seem to have seen the inside of a stadium in a long time. More of a bookworm and a nerd, he lacked the motor skills to shine in a sport.

"The ground," someone shrieked from the back of the class.

"Yes, Sherlock, that is where you need to be for the tryouts. Don't be late." The boy left for lunch break. He looked like he needed to eat a bit more every day—or at least eat more greens.

Gopal, Ram, Ali, and the other four boys all got selected in the starting eleven to play the match.

Everyone had a big smile painted on their faces, including the girls who joined the trip at their own expense.

"Hyderabad is a new city," said Rocky. Never one to have all the details correct, Rocky was blurting out half-baked information.

"No, stupid. Telangana is the new state of which Hyderabad is the capital city. I hear that there is still a little political unrest over there."

The nine of them packed their suitcases and got ready for the trip. Anticipation thrilled them as they waited to start their journey.

The school had hired a van to take them to Hyderabad, which was not exceedingly far away and would take a day to reach.

"Back to the political scenario, elections are going on over there now."

"I'm a little concerned about that as well, but what can we do now?"

They sang, played games, slept, and even quarreled during the journey, but what they did not expect was that the van would break down before they arrived.

They had reached three-quarters of the journey on the road to Hyderabad, and there was no one on the freeway they could hail or stop.

It was also raining.

"Great. Just great. This is just what we need at the moment. My cricket kit is getting ruined."

"Don't cry about it. Enjoy every minute. Your bag is waterproof."

The door of the van needed oil. It croaked like a frog every time someone tried opening it. Carrying the umbrella, the teachers and students filed out.

There were potholes on the road. The puddles of water needed to be circumvented carefully. Rocky liked to jump into them. One look from the girls, and he stopped. The thirteen, along with the teachers who were accompanying them, trudged along.

"I...err...I need.... Can you come a little closer, teacher?" Ram looked uncomfortable, like he was sitting on a pot of boiling water.

"What do you need, Ram?" The teacher brushed the sweat from her face. The moisture coupled with the heat of the sun was doing no one any good.

Everyone was happy to see the rainbow, though. Like the northern lights, it looked gorgeous. The violet color was prominent, as if someone had painted a picture on the sky.

"Sir, I need to use the loo." Ram blushed with embarrassment.

"Go on the side of the road." The teacher was practical. It was not an uncommon sight in certain places of the world. The facilities were limited compared to the size of the population, and the poor were always the most affected.

"It is not a bathroom." Ram was flabbergasted. He knew the ways of the world. Yet, the words coming from his favorite teacher bothered him.

"Holy Krishna." The teacher rolled her eyes. She had dyed her hair black. The speckles of white were still peeping out like the stars in the night sky. She could not hide her age.

There was a sugarcane field close by. Ram made a dash to the fields. The leaves were his toilet paper. He realized that he was closer to nature then than he had ever been before. Like camping out in the woods during the lean season.

At last, a bus stopped and picked them up. The bus was painted bright-green to attract the attention of travelers. It did the job well.

The teachers paid for themselves and the boys, while the girls paid out of their own pocket. Not long after, they reached Hyderabad.

"This is a beautiful place. I don't mind it here at all," said Gopal. He looked at ease. *I don't feel the heat here much,* he thought.

"That is because land surrounds us on all sides, and there's no moisture in the air. So, we shouldn't sweat much," Ram said, as if he could decipher Gopal's thought process.

"Ha. Lucky people." Gopal was genuinely jealous. "Do you know how sweaty it can get near the ocean?" A landlocked area with less moisture was a blessing in disguise.

"The sun and the dry heat over here are not as healthy as it is in Chennai. We might sweat over there, but at least that helps our skin. On the downside, mosquitoes breed more over there. There is a balance we need to strike, and losing one disadvantage can gain us another," said Leela. She was listening intently to the conversation.

"You are the boss, and if you say it, then it must be true. Oh, well. Not everyone can have everything, can they?" Ram shrugged. He was matter-of-fact.

They stayed in four service apartments with three bedrooms each. Each person shared rooms with one or two other people. The girls took a room for themselves.

The rooms were not fancy. Paint was peeling from the ceiling and walls. The smell of cats wafted toward them. Strays were a common nuisance there.

The wet dogs were worse. They barked and chased the cows and cars. Joggers had to make sure that they did not look like they were running from the hounds in order to not attract the canines' attention and encourage them to give chase.

The chef gave them an early breakfast, and then they explored the city. They traveled to Shilparamam, which was in the heart of HITEC City.

There were many attractions there, and the theme of olden-day India that dominated the area impressed them. The well-maintained huts, the music, pottery, et cetera, were a treat to the eyes.

"Historical places and museums. What a wonderful trip we have had so far," Gopal muttered.

"Sleep, yawn, fall down on the ground—what a wonderful companion you are," mocked Leela.

"Will you two give it a rest?" Ram remarked.

"Look who's talking—it is the sugarcane guy." Gopal punched his fists together.

Ram got angry and biffed Gopal's face. Gopal's entire jaw rattled, and he fell to the ground.

Ram felt ashamed that he had lost control over such a trivial matter. The rest of the team gathered around the pair, and the teachers looked at Ram with shock. They did not expect Ram, of all the kids there, to throw a punch at his friend. Ram looked down to avoid their gazes.

Even Leela reeled back at the sudden violence, but she helped Gopal to his feet.

"I'm sorry, Gopal," Ram said. "I should have controlled myself." Ram's voice was so weak he could not hear himself. Gopal got the point, though.

"It was my fault. I should not have instigated your anger. I'm sorry too." Gopal spoke in a low but clear voice. It was not the physical pain that bothered him.

"Give each other a hug," instructed Ram's teacher.

The boys inched their way toward each other. Looking down to avoid eye contact, they gave a cursory hug and even patted each other on the back.

"That's it, and don't repeat it again," the teacher cautioned.

"Teacher, I think he broke half of my tooth. I can kind of feel it, but it's not hurting me. It's just that the tooth is crumbling down, and there is no better word for it." Gopal was fingering his tooth.

Ram felt guilty. From there, they made their way to a dentist's clinic. The entire cricket team, the two girls, and the teachers crowded into the clinic, concerned for Gopal. The receptionist was wide-eyed.

"What do you think this place is?" she scolded. Without waiting for a reply, she continued, "We allow only the patient and one attendant. The rest of you can wait outside. We can't let you parade up and down in here." She stood up and placed her hands on her hips, frown lines on her forehead.

"What happened?" asked the dentist. "How did you break your tooth?"

"I fell down," lied Gopal before anyone could say anything. Ram felt a gush of gratitude.

The kids trampled the carpet as they streamed out of the one-story building.

"It is all right. There is no pain."

"I understand that you're still a child, but to have a tooth broken at this young age is not okay. I will take care…matter of fact, I will give you a temporary solution, but when you reach your hometown, you must get a filling."

"What is a filling? Does it hurt a lot?"

"Don't worry about that. Just know that your teeth will look normal after you get the filling. It is just going to replace the other half of the tooth you lost."

With that, the doctor flushed out the loose tooth particles by using a jet of water. Gopal felt ticklish, and he smiled with his mouth already wide-open, making him look like a goldfish who swallowed a golf ball.

After an hour, they left the clinic.

"Teacher, we've had a tiring day. Can we go home and take a rest now? I feel sleepy, and I never want to get up again. Today wore out my legs, and my entire body is struggling to stay awake."

"Rocky, I think we've had enough for one day. I believe that you're right. We better head home now. Sightseeing can wait till tomorrow, and then it's down to business soon. Play to win, folks."

So, they returned to the service apartment and walked up the stairs to their rooms.

"Anyone know why we're walking upstairs and not taking the elevator? I don't think this is the time for exercising. I'm already dehydrated, exhausted, and I don't want to walk anymore. This heat is making my blood evaporate."

Some guys laughed.

"There is no electricity, dummy. You think we would climb stairs otherwise?"

"I thought there was a generator in here. Didn't the watchman turn it on yet?"

They reached the room, and the boys gulped down the water.

"Ah, water, the elixir of life…"

"Do you know where the main switchboard is?"

"Why do you ask?"

"We need to turn on the switch that'll shift from standard current to generator power."

"Okay, no problem. I know where it is, and I will get it done."

Everyone slept that night. The next day, at early morning, the teachers woke everybody up. They had their breakfast and boarded the bus.

There was a huge billboard that read: "Kids' fair is now open," and all the children wanted to go to the event. Soon enough, that was where they were heading.

"How much for the entrance ticket?"

"It is Rs. 30 for the kids and Rs. 50 for an adult ticket."

"Our gang consists of thirteen children." The teacher looked around to confirm the number. Once she was sure, she said, "And three adults, please."

"Thank you for giving us the change, because we need it. We have a long day ahead of us." The man was in his mid-fifties and wearing a bright red cap. "Would you like a white, red, black, or blue cap for the children? It is complimentary with the ticket."

"It's hot, and so I think going with the white hat is the best option. Other shades are not good enough."

It was a crowded day, and the children enjoyed the activity zone, where they saw blown-up balloons that resembled their favorite characters, like the Iron-man and the Hulk.

They jumped up and down on the trampoline with other kids and enjoyed themselves. The trampoline was in constant motion, not allowing the kids to stop even if they wanted to. They had to jump all the way if they wanted to get out.

There was an inflatable castle from which the kids could start at the top and slide all the way down. By the time the children had tried out all the rides, they were starving.

The hall was air-conditioned, so the group felt like they were in a cool valley, but still hungry. The hours passed, and then they made their way to the food court. They waited in line to get their tasty food. Since most of them were vegetarian, it didn't take the vendor long to prepare any of it.

"Rocky, why are all these people wearing masks? It looks as though they are going to a doctor's conference. Is there an epidemic going on?"

"I believe so. I think it's called the swine flu, and it seems to be most prevalent in Hyderabad compared to the rest of the cities in India."

"Why are we not getting the masks?"

"I guess we will get some." And soon enough, when they left the kids' show, each kid got a Rs. 10 mask that lasted about three days maximum. They figured that by that time they should be back home with a medal or two.

"This is a good workout session for us, and I already feel flexible and ready to kick someone's backside in tomorrow's match."

"That is the spirit. We can do it."

They had pleasant dreams that night and none, by the grace of God, had any nightmares. Rocky was dreaming of the fruits they brought along. Food was a constant thought in his mind.

For better protection, they wore the masks, feeling as if they were surgeons about to operate on their next patient. The visitors left the rooms before the sun had come out. Since they could not have their breakfast that early, they each had a green banana and started their day.

The Incident

They reached the cricket pitch long before the opposing team arrived. They did their warm-ups and jogged around the field. The children waved their hands, jumped up and down, bent and touched the ground without bending their knees, and other such exercises. By that time, the sun had broken through the wavy morning clouds. Beads of sweat were trickling down the face of each player.

The Chennai team wore green shirts with yellow stripes, which caused Leela's eyebrows to go up.

"What a dress sense! Even clowns and buffoons wear better costumes," Leela teased.

"Ha, ha. Amusing! Thanks for that." Gopal shrugged.

"You are most welcome," she said with a sweet voice and a mocking bow. "I am already sleepy. When is the match going to start? This is so boring."

"We will start in another ten minutes, once the umpires come. Once they arrive, they will call the captains to do the coin toss, and the winner will have to choose between batting and bowling."

It was like Laurel and Hardy had arrived. The two umpires were two extremes in weight. One was plump and cheerful-looking, while the other looked as if he had not eaten in days. The thin umpire was wearing a tight shirt that outlined his ribs. The other umpire was dressed in a plain red t-shirt with a blue collar and wore a matching red cap and dark-blue jeans.

"Here goes nothing," said Ali, and he walked to the center of the pitch, where the two umpires and the opposing captain were waiting.

"What do you choose? Heads or tails?" asked the plump umpire.

"I choose heads," said Ali.

He tossed the coin, and it landed on the ground. It fell with the head facing upward.

"You win. What do you choose? Do you wish to bat, or do you prefer to bowl?"

Ali had decided before he came to the pitch what he would do if he won the toss. He had discussed it with his coach and his teammates the previous evening.

"I'll bowl."

The team arranged themselves on the field. It was an aggressive fielding set-up, with several fielders close to the batsmen to catch the ball when it nicked the bat. The new ball swung with ease, and they were hoping to get as many wickets as possible.

Ali, the captain, was the opening bowler. He was a medium-pace bowler who could swing the ball like someone had made it out of plastic.

"Everybody ready?" he called out loud, and there were general nods from the fielders. He took thirteen steps from the crease and marked the point from where he would like to take the run-up.

"Right arm over the wicket," cried the umpire.

There was excitement in the air, and the bowler ran. The hands of the umpire came up and stopped Ali midway.

A dog was running on the pitch. The batsman swung at the dog, and it yelped and ran away with its tail between its legs.

The fielders clapped to encourage the bowler once again to gather his momentum.

It was a yorker and darn-near dislodged the batsman from his feet.

"Good ball," yelled Ram from the outfield.

In the first ten overs, only one wicket fell, and the opponents had scored at a run rate of 5.5 per over. They called a tea break and drank juice and chatted for five minutes.

"I'm already tired and weary." Gopal dragged his feet across the turf.

"It is the sun. It's too freaking hot." Rocky was not cheerful at all.

"I have a major problem." Gopal sounded apologetic.

"What is it? What happened?" Ram was concerned. Gopal was not one to complain.

"My shoes are new, and they are squeezing my toes. I don't think I can continue playing. It feels as though my leg is being chewed up by a piranha. I'm dying of pain, here." Gopal was clearly uncomfortable.

"We cannot do it without you," said Roger, who was a lanky young boy. He had short hair that tapered in the sides. He looked like a man from the youth army. "You are the best fielder there is. Just five more overs. It will be over in no time. You mark my words."

"I can't do it, Roger. I wish I could," replied a deflated Gopal.

"Hold on a second. I think I have an old pair of shoes that just might fit you. Why don't you try them?"

Roger fiddled with his kit, and after a while pulled out an old pair of well-maintained shoes. He gave them to Gopal, who took them with gratitude and tried them on.

"These feel like I am floating on a cloud. Are you sure you want to loan them?"

"Why not?"

"Thanks a ton, buddy."

"No problem. Don't mention it."

They bowled the next thirty balls with high tension. Ali's team tried to make sure that the other team did not make too many runs.

Two more wickets fell, but that did not stop them from hitting a hundred runs.

"We are goners. I'm sure they will win unless Ram and Roger pull off a miracle for us."

There was a twenty-minute break during which the boys suited up.

"All right. Everyone on the field."

"Here we go. This is it."

The team chanted, "OO-AAH-OO-AAH-ASKALAKADI-KALAKA LAKIDI-OO-AAH-OO-AAH."

Chewing on a stick of gum, Ram waited for the bowler to take the long run-up. On the new end of the pitch, Roger was fidgeting.

The first ball was a bouncer and aimed at Ram's chest, but Ram took advantage of the situation and played an unorthodox shot, sending the ball over the boundary line.

The team back in the pavilion was hooting, and Leela screamed, "We need another one, just like the other one. That was a jolly good one!"

When the applause died down, Gopal and Ali retreated to the shade of a nearby tree and played catch.

"Gopal, you better suit up. You will be next."

In the meantime, Roger was making sure that the runs kept trickling in with the ones and twos. It gave Ram the opportunity to take the risky shots for the first few hours, and when he ran out of steam, Roger would take over. That was the plan, and they stuck to it.

Gautham was keeping track of the score.

"What is the score now, Gautham?" asked Leela.

"We have hit 23 runs, and they have given us four extras. That makes 27 runs."

"How many overs?"

"3.5 overs."

"That's a good run rate."

Leela turned and walked away. Gautham did not understand why Rocky screamed, "Twinkle, twinkle, little star...my friend Ram is a superstar. Gautham adds four more runs to the score. That was a splendid shot. Straight drive."

The next ball was a good-length ball but a little off the stumps, and so Ram nicked the ball to the third man. Roger ran, but Ram hesitated, and that cost him his wicket.

A new bowler came, and a new over began, with Gopal at

the batting end.

Thud!

Gopal stopped the fast-paced ball in its tracks by a solid defensive stroke. The second ball of the over, Gopal hit it for six. The ball landed on a rainwater harvesting tank, getting wet.

That gave the bowler an opportunity to shine the ball on the one side and leave the ball rugged on the other.

That was when some loud music played; it had a somber vibe to it. The players watched a set of people march down the road next to the playground.

"I forgot that there was a cemetery next to the playground."

The lady in front was sobbing and beating her chest. The sight brought tears to the onlookers' eyes.

"Ready?" yelled the bowler, bringing the batsman's attention back to the scene at hand. Gopal prepared himself for the next ball.

With a vengeance, the bowler swung the ball, which skidded on the pitch and struck Gopal in the genitals. Gopal screamed for just a fraction of a second before he crumbled to the floor and lay motionless.

Everyone rushed to him; they shrieked and poured water on him, but to no avail. The boy remained motionless. Everything seemed to stand still for a second. Not even the sweat was running down his face.

"Call the ambulance."

There was panic and pandemonium around Gopal. Ram was by his friend's side, looking helpless.

The teachers rushed to the pitch. They were scared to let anything happen on their watch. Their thoughts were on their careers.

The bowler was scared he would be jailed if anything serious had happened to Gopal. The bowler was a year older and a meat eater. Gopal was a vegetarian and meek in comparison.

"He is not breathing. Give him mouth-to-mouth," Rocky screamed.

He is breathing, thought Ram. He did not have the notion of correcting Rocky. Gopal's eyes were white—the pupils weren't visible. He looked too much like a corpse.

Where is the ambulance? Roger thought, looking around to see what was taking so long.

It was no use. Gopal died on the spot, breathing his last in Ram's hands. "Gopal," Ram called. "Are you with me, buddy?" The tears rolled uncontrollably.

"I saw him remove his abdomen guard; he had been complaining it was always itching him. Now he is dead because of it." Gautham was in shock.

"There is nothing we can do for him now. He is with the good Lord, and may He protect him from all evil. This is a terrible way to die, and I feel so sorry for him."

"The tremendous pain he must have undergone. I can't imagine. Poor boy. No one deserves to die this way, not a person like him."

Ram was deeply sorrowful and felt guilty about hitting him a day or two ago. How could he have been so harsh to such a sweet boy?

A popcorn packet drifted nearby and seemed to pass by,

making no noise; Roger kicked it to let off some steam.

"Who the bloody hell bowled this ball?" Ram was furious.

"Listen, it was not intentional. We could never have predicted that he would not protect himself when coming onto the field. Don't fault the bowler just because you want somebody to blame."

"How dare you? You are putting the blame on Gopal? If you didn't play an aggressive game and hadn't bowled to bodyline him, then this would never have occurred. You remember that."

"This is just a game."

"Calm down. We can't do anything now."

"Argh."

Everyone turned their attention to Leela. She had fainted and hit her face on the bat that was lying down on the ground. Her face immediately began swelling up, and blood began to pour out of her, but her eyes remained shut. She was moaning in pain.

The blood was redder than the setting sun and thicker than tomato sauce. It made Ali a little dizzy.

"Leela...Leela." A streak of fear flashed across the face of coach Arjun. "What is happening over here? Everything is going wrong today. When will the Godforsaken ambulance arrive? I'm tired of waiting. Is this an emergency or not?"

The ambulance arrived five minutes later. The medical staff took control of the situation. They took Gopal in the ambulance, and the coach followed with Leela in his car.

They flew past the vehicles on the road and got through the red lights with no issues. The siren was blaring, and the noise screamed "URGENCY" to everyone in the vicinity.

The vehicles came to a halt in the emergency section of the hospital, where the medical staff got down and took the boy to the ICU. They were trying to restore life to Gopal's body.

Coach Arjun put the semiconscious Leela in the wheelchair and drove over to the receptionist.

"What's wrong?"

"She fainted from shock and walloped her head on a cricket bat on the pitch."

"Take her to the third floor on the "B" Wing and look for room 303. She will be cared for. Give us some time, please?"

"Thank you. And what about the boy in the ICU? Can I see him?"

"First things first, attend to the young lady and then come for the boy."

He wheeled her to room 303; the doctor came in ten minutes after they arrived and introduced herself as Dr. Shanthi. After seeing the girl's condition, the doctor said, "She has wounded herself, but I will give her something to calm her nerves and apply balm to the wound. We have to wait for it to heal."

A small movement. A flutter of the eyes. Leela moaned. She was becoming aware of her surroundings. She had heard the conversation.

"I am already a patient," Leela joked. But she was not fooling anyone. They could see the anguish she was going through at the loss of Gopal.

The doctor left, closing the door gently behind her. She had seen many a tragedy occur at the hospital. She would not allow herself to grow numb because of it, though.

"Hello," a cheerful voice cried out from somewhere in the room.

That startled the coach and the girl out of their wits. They turned around to see who had called out.

An old man was sitting up in the bed semi-partitioned from view on the other side of the room.

"Hello." Leela was cautious.

"My name is Karthikeyan. What are your names?"

"I am Arjun, a cricket coach. This is a student who studies at the school I work at, and her name is Leela."

"That is a beautiful name: Leela. I have a granddaughter with the same name. You know what the name means?"

"No, Uncle. I don't."

"Nor do I." And he laughed. "What is ailing you, my dear?"

"I fainted." She looked down. "My friend died today. I witnessed the whole thing, and that is when I fell down and hit my face on a cricket bat that was resting on the ground."

"That is regrettable."

"What is wrong with you, Uncle?"

"Just a case of dehydration. I, too, fainted. I'm getting too old. I travel a lot, by foot at times. And I fell because my body couldn't take it." The old man looked like he had been starving for days. His bones were visible, but his tone was rock-solid.

Coach Arjun checked on Gopal and left Leela and the old man to speak with each other.

Within minutes, Leela poured out her entire story and background. The old man took pity on her and told her that there was a way to get Gopal back.

"You're joking, right? He is dead. The doctors are trying to revive him, but I know that he will not come back."

"There is a way to make him live again." And then he told her the story about the nine mysterious men and the books of power.

"How do you know that the story is true?"

"I am the heir of the boy that Raza saved."

"Why are you telling me all this?"

"This is no secret. Only the worthy can find the book of power. I've told many people about this story, and only a few individuals have believed me. Whether you choose to believe me or not is up to you."

That evening, the whole gang left for the airport. They arrived late. The manager on duty was Mr. Raghul, who mixed his words all the time.

He was a short, stout, nearly bald man with thick glasses and a dark complexion.

He looked the coach in the eye and said, "This time, I am allowing you, but the next time you bring your body late, I will not accept it." He left a shocked coach behind in his wake.

However, the trip was uneventful, and they reached

Chennai in one hour's time. Seeing the parents would be hard, the coach knew. As soon as the casket was visible, Mr. and Mrs. Niketan howled with agony.

Roger's father, Mr. Jonathan, came over to give his condolences before taking his son back to Kilpauk, where they lived.

They transported the dead body to Adyar, where the nine children resided. On the way home, it rained as if the world was crying for losing this young life. Gopal's body and his parents were in the car, heading home. As they stopped at the red light, the parents saw an ambulance pass by with blaring sirens. Mrs. Niketan prayed for the patient in that ambulance, who might be fighting for his life.

As they neared home, the car got stuck in a big pothole in the road. They got out, cursing the infrastructure.

The economy of India was booming, but still, the infrastructure needed improvements to sustain the vast population present in the country.

They carried the body and the casket the rest of the way, and the eight remaining children helped lift their friend, who weighed a little more than they expected. This was their way of paying their respects to their lifelong childhood friend.

For two days, they kept the body in the home for relatives from across the country to come and see their beloved family member. At the end of the second day, they carried the body to the graveyard, where they cremated him.

The grieving parents got in their car and left the cemetery. They were driving fast when one of their tires burst, causing them to skid all over the place. It did not injure them, and they called for some assistance.

For the next couple of days, everything seemed quiet. Then, Lakshmi came back to her home and made a special request. She was unlike Leela. She had a mole on her forehead that some said was a sign of great intelligence. She was part of the gang, smart and capable. She had recently gone on a vacation but had heard what happened to Gopal and rushed back, lest they burn the body before her arrival.

The remaining eight friends gathered together in the evening at Gopal's residence. Lakshmi was a graceful dancer, and she danced to a sad number. They knew her for her Bharatanatyam, and her expressions conveyed what she was undergoing at the loss of her friend. It was nothing short of spectacular.

She was not dancing to any pre-recorded music; Kumar was playing the flute. He drew a long breath and played on, melting the hearts of his listeners.

At the end of the dance, Gautham got up and spoke. "Gopal loved riddles, and he was great at answering them. There was a question he had asked me that I can still remember. I will ask the same to you all now:

There was a man named Demon and another called God. God always told the truth, and the Demon always used to lie. There was a fork in the road, where the two men stood. You could only ask them one question. Then, you would have to choose which way leads to heaven and which one leads to hell. What is the question you would ask?"

There was silence as they pondered the question. Then, Mrs. Niketan came up with the answer:

"If I were to ask the other person which road points to heaven, what will the answer be?"

"You are as good as your son at solving riddles."

"I have another one he had asked me not too long ago: I was on my way to Saint Ives. I crossed the path of seven wives. Every wife had seven sacks, and every sack had seven cats. Every cat had seven kittens. So, kittens, cats, sacks, wives, how many went to Saint Ives?" Ali blurted it out fast.

It rocked the others for a second, and then they snorted; only Gopal could have come up with such interesting questions.

They had to ask Ali to repeat himself twice or thrice before they got all the variables right.

"Seven to the power seven?"

"No."

"How about seven factorials?"

"That is not the answer either."

"This guy was going to St. Ives, while the rest were coming in the opposite direction. So, the answer is: one. Am I correct, Ali?"

"You got it, Ram."

They were about to leave when Mrs. Niketan said, "It was fun to have you all over here. I will feel a little lonely without the voices of children in the house. Would you all like to spend the night over here, perhaps?" She tried to control her sobbing but was unsuccessful.

The kids were not sure if it was prudent to stay in a house where there had been death. It would be awkward without their friend around. They would have to maintain a level of seriousness that was not natural for the children.

"We will have to ask permission first, Aunty. We will be

back in a few minutes after telling our parents. Otherwise, maybe we can use the intercom in this apartment?"

"Sure, that is a good idea. I don't want to impose anything on any of you. If you would rather go home, I understand."

"Nothing like that, Aunty." Lakshmi gave Mrs. Niketan a hug.

They stayed over at Gopal's house for the night and gave Aunty their company, and she shed a tear over it.

They bundled up on the floor and talked late into the evening about the adventures they had had with Gopal. Mrs. Niketan then retired to the bedroom, leaving the children alone.

"I have news for all of you." Leela's eyes were gleaming with fever and enthusiasm. "I can bring Gopal back to life."

"Have you lost your senses? I threw Gopal's ashes in the sea, and you can't bring that back. I don't want to be pessimistic or rude, but it is high time we recognize that our beloved friend is no more," Rocky burst out with tears in his eyes.

Leela did not mind the rudeness. She could well understand what he must be going through.

"I am not crazy, and I understand the situation, but I have something to share with all of you…." And she spoke for an hour, describing what the old man had told her about the book of power, as her companions listened in rapt silence.

Once she finished, Rocky, skeptical as usual, said, "His dehydration has left him crazy, and you believe him too?"

"I may not believe him, but I want to. If there is even a glimmer of hope in getting him back… We must try, at least."

They agreed to discuss this further later on. It tired the kids, and it was too late in the night or too early in the morning, and they had to sleep.

The next day, the other kids tried to discourage her from the concept of reviving Gopal, but she was adamant.

"If you guys are not willing, then I will try this on my own. I need nobody. I thought we were all friends, and we would give anything for each other…would have been helpful to know earlier that you guys would ditch at the first instance of trouble."

"This is not like, you know, we are abandoning you, or anything like that. This is us talking sense into you. There aren't any flying chariots or horses." It exasperated Kumar.

"This is not Santa Claus we are talking about. Ramayana. Hello? This is the stuff of legends. Perchance the Wizard of Oz copied the "monkeys flying" idea from us, but hey, we have a historical document that proves that there was a person named Ram, and he was—"

"See, I don't want to argue with you. We will play along, for your mental peace of mind. Are you happy now?" Rocky asked.

"I agree with Rocky," said Ram, and that was the end of the conversation. Leela was beaming with happiness.

There was no school that day. The children were allowed to stay home so they could properly grieve over the loss. It was their way of mourning the death of one of their students.

Kumar was on his way to see his friends when his mother called out, "Are you…have you taken your hanky?"

"I don't need it, Ma."

"Never leave home without it," she retorted. Kumar made a face but took the hanky she handed him before leaving the house.

"What shall we do today? Can we plan? Yes, that's it. We need a plan. Let us discuss…"

"Okay, Leela. Let's do this: We will meet after lunch again at my place, and we'll talk about what to do next."

They all had a hurried lunch in their respective homes and then helped clean their tables.

When they met at Ram's place, it was well past two p.m., and Ram's mother, Divya, was snoring away to glory, while his father was at the office.

"We open this session for a discussion on the ways to get these so-called books of power written by the nine mysterious men. Anyone who has any ideas are welcome to share their thoughts. We need someone to keep the minutes of the meeting."

"I can do that." Ali was already reaching out for a pen and paper.

"So, let's begin by going through what the old man said to Leela."

"Raza was going south with the book…."

"He was a communications expert but had the book of anti-gravity."

"He rescues a poor boy out of miserable conditions…"

"Okay, got it. Enough! I'm sure everyone remembers. Now, what is the plan?" Leela interrupted.

"We need to raise funds. Nothing happens without cash in

the pocket. The deeper the pockets, the further we go in our quest. We need to think of a way to ask our parents for money."

"No! This is our quest, and we must not bother nor involve them. Promise you will not include them at any cost."

They all promised Ram, who then plotted on how to get money.

"There are online websites that deliver grocery items to doorsteps in parts of India. It is not available in Chennai. Why don't we do the same service for a nominal fee in our locality? Adyar is a big place, and rich people live here. This is the best location for starting this venture."

Gautham gave his two cents. "We will call this: Operation Vegetables."

"What if they want us to buy meat?" Kumar inquired.

"We are vegetarians and have knowledge about buying vegetables but know nothing about selecting good meat, and so we will stay away from that sector."

"I will get the website running. What shall we call it? Has everyone agreed on Operation Vegetables?"

They all nodded. It conveyed the message that the children would not deliver meat at any cost.

They were operating in full swing, and by the end of the week, there was a huge demand for this service.

People who were too busy or handicapped or just plain lazy used this option.

Once school restarted, they only had time to conduct business in the evenings, but they managed schoolwork and their business affairs.

"You won't believe what I read in one guy's apartment," began Lakshmi, smiling. "This guy is from the humor club, and I had gone to his house to deliver the goods, and on his front door he had written: I am the master of my house, and I have my wife's permission to say so."

The boys did not laugh, but the girls giggled. "Don't take it serious, guys. It will be your turn soon enough." And they laughed harder.

By the end of the first month, they counted the money they had collected so far.

"We have about Rs. 5000 in our kitty. Now, will it be enough for our next step?"

"That is a million-dollar question. There is simply one way to find out, and if we are short, then we will have to improvise."

The next weekend, they walked to the bus stop and bought tickets to Thiruvarur so they could see one of the biggest and tallest chariots in the world.

They planned to stay for two days and one night.

"What are we going to say to our parents?"

"I don't know."

"I think it is best we say nothing. We will be back the same day, right?"

"No, it will be for two days."

"That is the maximum time we would take, and I think we will be back on the same day. If we leave early and come back a little late, it will be smooth sailing. No problem."

Early on Saturday morning, the guys got up and left, just

like that, informing no one about anything.

"Ram," screamed Divya, his mother. "Come out of your room. It is time for lunch already. How long are you going to sleep today?" Divya knocked and entered the room, but there was no sign of Ram.

"Did you see Ram go out today?" she asked her husband. "Because I cannot find him."

"He must have gone to play with the other kids," he consoled her.

The doorbell rang twice.

"Have you seen Gopal?" Mrs. Niketan's face was tear-streaked. "He goes nowhere without telling me, and he seems to be missing this morning. I thought I would scold him when he returned, but he has not so far, and I am getting worried."

"He is not with us anymore, remember?"

"I have been having too many pills. I can't forget. I am unable."

"That is fine, dear. Ram is not there in his room. We should check with the others and see where he is."

The two concerned mothers left to search for Ram and knocked on doors to see if Ram was with another family. The eight children's parents were soon at the police station, reporting their lost children.

They gave photographs of their children to the police officers and all other necessary information.

"Once again, just to check if I am right: These kids have been working for the past month to earn cash, but you do not know how much they made?" The parents shook their heads. The policeman continued, "This is odd behavior. Okay, we can wrap it up for the night, now. We will get in touch with you if we have updates."

The parents acted like their seats were red-hot; they could not sit tight in one place. Soon, they ventured to the railway station and asked the ticketing person if they saw eight children without adults buying tickets from there.

"No, sir, I have no recollection of seeing these kids."

They went to all the ticketing counters and checked them one by one. They waited in the queue in every stand till their turn came to question the ticketing staff.

Anyone could see the love they had for their children. Anyway, getting on with the story, they went to the bus stops next. It was late in the night by now, and only the staff member whose shift had just ended was still present. He was leaving when the parents rushed forth and told her their story and showed the pictures.

"I saw them. I think they were on the bus for Trichy or someplace. You can check the camera."

And when they checked, they found that the children had boarded the bus going to Thiruvarur. This sudden move by their children flabbergasted them. They were scratching their heads.

"Half of us will stay back, and half will proceed to Thiruvarur to find the children. Does that sound like a full-fledged plan?"

They decided on it, bought the tickets, and boarded the night bus. They were in luck.

The remaining parents made their way back to the police station to update the officers on everything they had learned that day. They informed the Thiruvarur police about the kids.

"Why a chariot? Why are we in Thiruvarur?" Gautham was a little confused. The city was an ancient one with rich history, a place where spiritually enlightened souls emerged. It felt as though seeds were sown in this holy place. The people were smart and kind. It was hot, just like any other city in the Province of Tamil Nadu.

"Brilliant, aren't you, to be asking this now, at the last minute? Read the myth, dummy. People are flying in chariots and shooting arrows at each other. This is the most famous one, so we are starting our search here. It is just a wild goose chase, if you ask me, but if it helps Leela find closure, then it is worth the trouble. Those chariots must have used the anti-gravity power to travel, and if this book is right, then this is a good place to start," John answered.

"But in that story of Raza, didn't the lion point toward the capital city, Madras?"

"Would you want anyone to know where you are hiding your lucky pencil? Yes, I know that you have one and that you protect it. Same way. If this Raza guy were a little smart, then he would not have listened to the lion's words. He got shortlisted in the most talented 'nine group' in the kingdom of Ashoka, and so it is logical to assume him to be a little smart and to hide it someplace else but still somewhere significant."

Police guarded the chariot, but it was such a tedious duty that the guard went off to snooze in the nearby hut.

A giant of a chariot, built for strength and stability, it was considered holy. It overshadowed everything close by.

The wheels were as big as that of an aircraft's, and the weight would have drowned the *Titanic* by itself.

The children sneaked in and searched high and low for the book. When they could find nothing, they lay there until they fell asleep.

In the morning, Rocky got up when someone punched him in the gut.

"Oi...kids, what are you doing here?"

Electrified with fear, the children scrambled away.

The guard was heavy and could not keep up. Rocky kept massaging his wretched gut.

The guard called his superiors at the police station, and they put the missing pieces together. His superiors showed the guard pictures of the kids, who recognized them immediately.

The police informed the parents right away. It thrilled them, though they were still puzzled as to the reason behind their strange behavior.

The kids went to the bus terminal, but their parents were waiting for them there.

Their parents' anger was reduced by the happiness of finding the children, but the kids still got an earful in the terminal. The public spectacle embarrassed the youngsters.

The parents bought the return tickets, and all of them returned on the next bus to Chennai.

When they got there, there was a second round of public blasting waiting for them.

The children took it all in good spirits, knowing that what they were doing was for their friend to find closure, and so they did not utter a word.

A week passed, and Ram was thinking about everything that had happened when he was met with a sad sight. A crow on the ground, unable to fly because of its broken wing, was scrambling to escape the jaws of a hungry cat.

Ram shooed the cat away, which tried to scratch him for denying it its meal, but it ran off.

He picked up the crow. It was too scared to do anything and was still like a statue in his hands.

Careful not to hurt it, he took it home and nursed it back to health.

From that day forth, they formed a bond, and the crow followed him everywhere, even to school.

"Coach, whose turn is it to bowl now? I finished my over. Can I bowl another spell?"

"It is the crow whisperer's turn to bowl. He is like Tendulkar at batting. He wants to try his hand at bowling. Hmm." Coach Arjun was skeptical about the idea.

The team was practicing in the nets as usual, but it felt weird to them to be playing without Gopal. He had been their wicketkeeper.

"Okay, time to wrap it up. Enough practice—go back to your studies this time."

The school realized that cricket was a good physical activity to occupy the children, who were the most affected by the loss of their friend.

A girl whom they had not noticed until just then walked up to them. Tall and dark with thin eyelashes, she had a look of superiority written all over her face and seemed confident. Some boys shuffled, not knowing what to do or where to look because looking right at her seemed too rude.

"This is my sister, and her name is Sheesha," said Roger as he patted her on the shoulder.

Since the boys were quiet, Lakshmi interjected, "Hey, pleased to meet you. My name is Lakshmi."

They smiled at each other.

"Are you done with the practice, Roger?" Sheesha questioned her brother and ignored the rest, who huddled closer to each other for some unknown reason.

"Yeah! Practice is over for the day."

"It was nice meeting you all," Sheesha said in a flat voice. She then turned and stalked off, her heels throwing up the mud that was loose.

Ram's phone rang, and that surprised the boys, who were eyeballing Sheesha's figure.

"Hello."

"Hi. Ram?"

"Yes?"

"This is Mrs. Niketan, Gopal's mom."

"Yes, I have this number saved."

"There is something I need to share with you and the rest of the children too. Can you come over? Is your practice done for the day?"

"Yes, Aunty! The practice is over for the day, and we will be there as soon as possible."

Ram kept his phone down.

He turned to the others and said, "That was Mrs. Niketan, and she said there was something she wanted us to see. We can go to her place straight from here and then go home. What do you guys say?"

They left for Gopal's home.

Mrs. Niketan was waiting on the balcony when they arrived. She saw them and went to open the front door. She was sweating under the fan.

"See this," she said, pointing at the computer monitor. "This email arrived from him."

It read:

Hi Amma,

If you are reading this, then it means I am no more. Though it is not the best situation, I don't want you to cry and stuff. It is all going to be okay.

There is a site that will forward my message after death to you.

They keep tabs on whether I am alive or not. If I don't reply to their inquiries, then they take it I am not alive anymore and then forward this message to you.

PS: I received a strange email today. It read: "Eight will find what the Nine have left behind."

The weird part was not the words—it was a self-destructive message. A month later, it will be deleted from the inbox automatically, as if it never existed. The message could not be copied or forwarded. Even a screenshot did not do the trick. Print was no use.

"He had edited that message two days before his death, and so this surprise email was recent. What do you think about it?"

"I don't know what to think. It was nice of Gopal to write to you from the spirit world, if I may be dramatic, but it was an accident the way he died. The bowler could not have predicted the ball would go in that line and length. He is not that good. Even international players aren't that good, as a matter of fact, but…I must accept that it is fishy."

"That is my thought."

"There is no point in pursuing it, though, Aunty. This is not a case of murder, as I just said."

She was quiet, but the sadness in her eyes pleaded for a better explanation of her only son's death.

Nobody else said a word, either. The children went to the terrace, and at once Leela pounced.

"I said so: nine of the secret men of Ashoka and eight of us. This fits. They meant us to save Gopal."

"It is very fishy. The circumstances are too coincidental for comfort. We need to make a greater attempt at solving this mystery, for Gopal's sake. We have to find what that message meant and why it went to him." Ram had not been onboard with this crazy idea from the get-go, but he reconsidered. "Did anyone have any strange or crazy or 'too wonderful to be true' moments in the past week?"

"I went to the mall last week."

"Nothing crazy about that."

"Let me finish, Rocky. As I was saying, I went to a shoe

shop and, as usual, was looking through the pairs I had most wanted for jogging, and there were only a couple left, so I bought them. When I asked for a discount, at first they said fifteen percent, and then, while checking out, their computer showed that this item was now on the promotional scheme and had a sixty-percent discount. It was awfully good to be true."

"Nothing too fishy about it." Rocky was trying to convince the others that nothing out of the ordinary was taking place.

"This might be nothing, but my mother went to a new salon, who gave her suntan lotion as a promotional gift for being the ninety-ninth customer...maybe the one-hundredth customer? Anyway, she gave me the lotion because I play out all the time, and she wanted it to protect me." Kumar kept it short.

"I have a strange tale to tell: I got up in the morning and, as usual, had my cup of milk without sugar for health's sake. Then my dad asked me to get the morning newspaper. I opened the door and, smack on top of the journal, there was a map." John paused for effect. "It was a map of Pakistan."

"What? Now you are spinning wheels here. I too received the same newspaper, and there was no insertion in it at all."

"That makes it odd, bozo."

The discussion continued in the school's cafeteria, and Roger heard some of it and found it fascinating.

Roger invited them over for ice cream.

"I like the way you think, Roger. Ice cream is a child's best friend," commented Gautham.

They had some hot chocolate, plus a cold cup of chocolate ice cream and mixed them both.

"Have you guys studied for the exams coming up?" Roger asked.

"We have other things in mind."

They told them about Gopal and the letter they had found.

Roger wanted to help in the quest to find the books of power, which Rocky had let slip to Roger.

Roger's father, Jonathan, was an alcoholic and an addict. He entered the ice cream shop unsteadily and caught hold of Roger by the scruff of his neck.

"Boy, you think you can buy ice cream with my money? I will not permit it." He hit Roger in the face. Ram tried to stop him, but Roger pleaded with Ram not to interfere.

Ram and the gang felt sorry for Roger as they saw him being dragged into the car and driven off by his personal driver.

"Poor guy."

"He will come over tomorrow."

"Why? It is Saturday tomorrow."

"He self-invited himself to my house to discuss the books of power, and he wants to fly away. I can understand why."

"Jeez."

The next day, Ram and the gang—along with Roger and a surprise guest, Sheesha—were sitting and discussing plans.

It was then that a bulb lit up in Gautham's head.

"It was the Kothanars."

"The who?"

"Don't you realize the significance?"

"What significance? What are you talking about? Make it clear for the rest of us, please."

"The Kothanars built a giant chariot like the one we had visited. This chariot is different because they dedicated it to the world-famous Thiruvalluvar."

"So," continued Gautham, "it is an amazing turn of events. Communications expert, Raza, brought the book to the chariot that we visited, but it moved to Chennai—identical to what the lion had said, but after its lifetime—and was placed in Valluvar Kottam."

"No way. That's so close. We can go to it right now."

They packed food and left in the car that Roger had come in. Squeezing ten children and an adult driver in one vehicle was no easy task, but the teens were lean.

Lo and behold, when they went there, hidden in plain sight was the book of power. The walls of the chariot had the key to the mystery. It was covered with wooden slabs as a part of the decoration. One of the slabs in the bottom was the book itself. This one was for anti-gravity.

There was just one teensy weensy problem: The book was written in a dialect they did not even understand a little.

"I have an idea." Leela fingered her chin. "Why not go to Asia's largest library? It is free for all, and we can check if this language is there, or we can ask the librarian if they have seen anything like this before."

"Brilliant. To the library, we go." Rocky was excited about

their progress.

The public transit took them across town, and they got off at the Anna Centenary Library in Kotturpuram.

"We need not ask the librarian what language this is. We need to know what language the people in the Kingdom of Ashoka spoke, and the probability of this being in the same language is high." Gautham pondered. "This must be in Urdu."

They headed to the aisle that had Urdu texts. They translated the book they had.

In the top right-hand corner of the right-hand page, they translated that word as "Urdu" in Urdu.

Gautham pressed that word and said "Urdu." The letters shone bright, and a drop-down box appeared with a list of various Indian languages.

"English translation is not here." Ram realized this was like in a computer where the words could be changed to different languages. This was a sophisticated book and an interactive one at that.

"They did not know English. Try Tamil."

The kids knew Tamil and had studied it for years in school. Tamil was one the of oldest languages in the world, and it was difficult to understand. They had a pretty good understanding of the English language, but it took them more time to read the words in Tamil.

It changed to Tamil. According to the instructions in the book, after speaking to "awaken" the chariot, commands can be given as to where it must go. Simple as that. No complications.

They looked at the chariot and then at the book. What to

do next? Where should they go from here? The story did not give a clue where the other books of power were, and there was no use awakening the chariot without knowing where they wanted to go from there.

"I got an idea." Rocky looked into Ram's eyes. "Why not use the clues given to us? The one with the Pakistan map—that is the only lead we have so far, and I say that—"

"That we go to Pakistan? Have you gone bonkers, buddy? We don't have a visa," replied Lakshmi, shocked.

"We don't need permits. The Pakistan government need not know that we are there."

"If they find out...? We will go to jail, won't we? This is too risky."

"A ship is safest in the harbor, but they mean it for the rough seas. I say we go ahead." Ram's determination was clear, and his words always carried a lot of weight with the children.

"So, do we start our business again?" Gautham was biting his nails.

"That will alert our parents to what we are about to do. That would be a stupid move." Ram looked at the magnificent chariot. "We only bought the tickets one-way. Some money must be left over. If I am right, there is about Rs. 1500 left. That is all we need. Gautham and John, I suggest that you take the money and buy supplies for our trip. We leave in another three hours' time."

John and Gautham went to the shop to buy food items.

Ram and the others reviewed the map of Pakistan while they drew up a plan. It showed an "X" near the border of Pakistan and India.

"At least we don't have to go too far into that country. We can get out with no one being the wiser."

They had started this hunt for the books of power to help Leela get closure over the death of Gopal, but now the entire situation had changed. They now did it with the purpose of bringing their friend back to life.

"Let's take the chariot for a spin."

"This is unbelievable. Where to now? Where in Pakistan are we going?"

"We are going to the Wagah border. That is where the map is pointing."

"The place where they do the 'lowering of the flags' ceremony?"

"Yup, that's the place we are heading to."

"Awesome."

Ram had gotten control of the chariot and had asked it to become invisible. It had not only become invisible but also became non-visible to hi-tech radar systems, which was a good thing since they wanted to cross international boundaries here. Obviously, the chariot was something that every country's armed forces would love to get their hands on.

They had flown through the clouds without a sound. No machinery grinded away within the apparatus. They could hear the world below them whispering to the sky above how much it longed to fly too.

"I am enjoying this very much." Rocky was trying to grab the clouds from the sky. "I wonder what will happen if I spit from the sky and it falls on someone's head?"

"Don't you dare."

"What will happen?"

"I think it will dissipate before it reaches the ground."

"It will evaporate?"

"Maybe dilute? I don't know for certain."

"Shall we give it a go, then?"

"How will we know if it has dissipated or not? Better not try it."

"What if I throw my water bottle down?"

"Rocky, stop it before someone gets hurt, and I am not talking about anyone on the ground."

The guys laughed. Leela could be a little intimidating at times. Ram's pet crow was right behind him. It never left his side. Ram was concerned. It needed to be with its own kind.

The chariot zoomed forward, and the crow that Ram had rescued fell back and could not keep up with the speed.

The invisibility aspect was tricky. But they managed it. No one could see where they were heading or where they landed.

They set their vimana down in time to see two army officers do their drill out in the open, close to the borders of their respective countries.

The kids joined the crowd of spectators and cheered for the Pakistani side. The Pakistanis were part of the same kingdom as the present-day Indians. They were our brothers and sisters.

The clean area took their breath away. Once the show was over, they dispersed with the outbound crowd.

"We can't take an auto rickshaw over here."

"Why not? Don't they have auto rickshaws over here? How do they commute? By bus?"

"Don't be an idiot. Can you not think of why we may not be able to get into an auto rickshaw?"

"Do we need a visa for that?" Rocky laughed.

"We don't have Pakistani currency, dummy."

"Oh."

"Okay," Ram said, watching as the sun set. "Let us move. Once we clear the area, we can decide where to go from there. We can walk. I don't expect it is too far off from here."

"Should we ask directions? What if we get lost?" Rocky was the embodiment of positive thinking, as always.

"Do you know Urdu?"

"Why would I know that?"

"You would have to know Urdu to talk to the locals. We need to get a little deeper into the country to talk our way in English. Not everyone here knows English. Just like India, the literate crowd knows English, and the rest speaks Urdu only."

"I heard that there is a village in Pakistan where they speak Tamil. I am not sure how true that statement is."

"Enough chatting. Where does the map say we need to head?"

"Who made you the boss, Leela, and why are you so impatient? We have come this far. We aren't going home without it, so relax."

A ten-minute walk later, they spotted a "Take Diversion" board. "There is a political meeting taking place over there, so we have to go around," said Ram.

Going around a crowd of thousands of people would normally take time and energy. They were in luck, though, since someone from the crowd was heading in the same direction and helped them get around the massive crowd.

They ended up on a lonely street that had a pungent smell of sewage. That was a shortcut, but halfway through, Leela threw up.

"I cannot take it anymore. I threw up on the new shoes I had bought. Can we not try to take an auto rickshaw, please?"

"You brought your new shoes?" Ram was not sure if he liked it or not. It could be a clue, but they were walking blind, and it could be a trap. They had not informed their parents as to their whereabouts for the second time in a row, even after getting punished the first time around.

Leela cried, "Do we need your permission for everything? This is my life, and I make my own choices, damn it."

"Cool down, sis. Ram is just trying to protect you. You got those shoes in circumstances out of the ordinary, that is all," Gautham soothed.

"You all take his side every time," screamed Leela. She was attracting attention from people on the streets.

"We will hail an auto rickshaw. Wait here, guys." It relieved Ram to get out of that tense situation. He knew that Leela was becoming quieter and more aloof, but it was driving him mad to see her mood swing over every little thing.

He tried to get an auto rickshaw, but none of them would accept his Indian currency. The three-wheeled vehicle was always moving in a precarious way. Foreigners liked them, as they thought it was an adventure to ride one. Bright yellow and green stripes across the vehicle made it pleasing to the eyes. This one used diesel and saved some money for the owner.

At last, they found a guy who would accept their money, and then they huddled in together.

"There are ten of us, plus the auto rickshaw driver. How are we going to get in? I know that this is a bigger vehicle than the regular ones, but it is ridiculous for us all to squeeze in."

"We have little choice. We either get in, or half of us walk or hail another auto rickshaw, or whatever. I don't see it as a good option. We will pay the guy extra for the trouble he is taking on our behalf."

The Indian currency was a little better than the Pakistani currency, but only just. It did not make a great deal of a difference.

Sitting on each other's laps and sandwiched, the kids had an uncomfortable ride.

The auto rickshaw driver took shortcuts to avoid being caught by the police with ten passengers. The kids were hanging onto the vehicle for dear life, as they were sitting halfway in the seats and halfway dangling out.

"Watch out," screamed Lakshmi, and the vehicle tilted over after a sharp turn.

The vehicle fell on them, but most of them cushioned the

fall for the rest, and it only bruised some. John, who was sitting in the front along with the driver, crashed onto the road hard and came close to breaking his ribs.

The iron bars had dug into John and caused him a little pain. His hands were bleeding, and he screamed louder from the impact with the ground than Leela, who was also doing her part of the screaming.

The bystanders called the police and the ambulance. They arrived fast.

They took John in the stretcher, and the ambulance with its sirens blaring led the way. The other children crowded into the police vans and followed John. Meanwhile, the auto rickshaw driver got arrested on the spot for breaking the rules.

The kids had paid the auto rickshaw driver for his troubles before boarding the police vans. He took it with a wry smile on his face.

The kids had minor bruises only. John landed in the government hospital.

"Where are the attendants?" Kumar was worried about his friend.

"There are other cases more urgent than John's, I suppose. You remember that this is a government hospital where many of the poor people who cannot afford healthcare come to visit. They must all have a lot on their hands as it is. I hope that someone comes soon, though. I'm happy they gave him painkillers."

When the doctor arrived, he examined him and diagnosed the problem as physical pain that would wear off in time, most likely in a day. Until then, he would have to take painkillers.

"If he is not in critical condition, why did they have to bring him in an ambulance in the first place?" Kumar was getting irritated with the medical staff.

The kids were further from their destination than they had planned in the beginning.

"Are you going to be all right, John?"

"Yeah, I already feel the pain receding. It was more of the shock than anything else. Had the iron rod dug deeper into me, then I would be in more serious condition, but thank God…"

"Allah has shown his infinite kindness to you, John." Ali closed his eyes and offered a quick *thank you* to God.

"We need to visit the police station." Ram looked determined.

"Do you want to spend the night in jail for visa fraud or something?"

"Keep your volume low, man. Do you want the entire country to know about our situation?"

"I want to get the auto rickshaw driver who risked everything out of jail. It is not fair on our part to leave him like that."

"And how do you propose that we pay for the penalty? Our currency is not worth two cents over here, remember?"

"We can't let that stop us from trying." Ram's determination won them over.

In the police station, they climbed the first flight of stairs and got to the guard in the reception area. "Excuse me, we are looking for…"

"English?"

"Yes."

"There." The guard pointed to another officer coming out.

"Excuse me, sir. I am looking for an arrested auto rickshaw driver, caught close to the Wagah border."

"It is Wagah on the Indian side and not on the Pakistan side."

"What's the difference?" blurted out Rocky before he could stop himself. He covered his mouth, not knowing if he had caused offense, and by the look he got from the police officer, he realized he was probably only escaping trouble because he was a child.

"Like I was asking..." Ram tried to bring the attention back to him and the main topic. "We are looking for—"

"Yes, he had been a reckless driver, but his wife has taken bail on his behalf. They are over there." Then, with a twinkle in his eye, he turned to Rocky, pronounced "W-A-G-H-A," and walked off.

"Oi," cried a woman's voice over the general discussion going on in the station. Everyone stopped to stare.

A puffed-up lady came to blast them in a language they did not comprehend. After a while, it became uncomfortable because she seemed to have asked a question and was waiting for a reply. The kids, not understanding a word of it, just gaped at her, which only fueled the lady's anger more.

The auto rickshaw driver came to their rescue. He pulled his spouse away, and she scoffed off. He apologized for her behavior.

"I hope you are like a baby with candy in his mouth, Ram?" Rocky was indignant. "We don't deserve this. Can we get out of here?"

"Sure" was all that Ram said.

"I hope they have insurance for their vehicle."

"I am not waiting around to ask her that." Rocky walked out of the police station, and the rest followed close behind.

Lakshmi could understand why Rocky was so irritated with them. Help the auto rickshaw driver? Rocky's glasses had come close to being broken, and the shards could have penetrated his eyes, making him blind. Not to mention the excruciating pain that would have lasted until they reached the emergency room of the government hospital.

"I am hungry," Leela said to Ram. "Is there something we can eat now?"

"Yeah! I think we will set up camp and have food."

They ate the food they had brought along with them. It was heavy, and some of it had gotten squashed during the fall, but everything was edible.

Sheesha made a lot of noise while munching on curd rice while a pickle was jutting out of her mouth. Her eating habit was disgusting to watch, and Lakshmi turned away.

Parents' Constant Worries

"Where the hell have these children gone off to now? Are they making a round trip to Tamil Nadu or what? And how did they get the money this time? Do you think they stole it?"

The barrage of questions only irritated Divya. "When I get my chance with that boy, he will wish he was never born," Divya muttered to herself. She was that cross. An hour later, when her anger had faded away, her concern for her child overtook her with overwhelming force.

"Do we go to the police this time?"

"What else do we do?"

Again, the band of parents walked to the nearby police station.

"The children have vanished again. We—"

"Do you think this is a game between you and your children, and if so, why are you bothering the police so many times? I am sure that the children have gone on another round trip and that they will be back when they run out of cash," the policeman replied with anger.

The parents wanted to lash out, but they were desperate, and they needed the help of this stupid man.

Just then, weird news came over the radio.

"They have spotted ten children flying a chariot. It is the Valluvar Kottam chariot that has gone missing."

The parents looked at each other. *That couldn't be right*, they thought. And even if it were true, bizarre as it may be, their children could not be the cause, could they?

The media had latched onto it. It was all over the news channel.

"This just in: A chariot is missing...and guess what, folks? Children are flying it."

It was hilarious for the parents to hear this, but they could not help but wonder what their kids were up to.

The internet had photos of the chariot flying—very vague pictures taken from phones that did not have a great camera built in.

The children had not discovered the invisibility portion of the book until a little while later.

"You can look on the TV for your kids, sir. Please leave," said the same rude policeman.

"Aren't you going to make a note of our complaint? This is unjust."

"Okay, okay. Give your complaint and leave. We will look into the matter."

They went home and turned on the TV. The reporter who was live said, "We are calling this the 'Houdini effect.' Who else could have accomplished this incredible task? There is no way this is possible. And people say the chariot flew. Not just a handful of people but an entire crowd of bus users are swearing by the story."

This time around, Roger and Sheesha's parents also lodged a complaint. The policeman had earned a little commission by tipping off the media about this.

"This just in. An unidentified source has confirmed that ten children have gone missing at the same time we saw the chariot flying. Coincidence? We don't think so. Let us know your comments by calling 1-800-chariot."

There was an online poll going on. The story had captured the hearts and imagination of many people, and those included not only children, but the adults were in on it too.

"Harry Potter craze," the media called it.

The doorbell rang, and Divya opened the door. The reporters invaded her space and questioned her about her kid.

"Do you think your children flew in the chariot?"

"Does your kid have magical talents?"

"Who taught them to fly?"

"Have they, by any chance, flown toy planes?"

The questions ranged from personal to bizarre.

Divya banged the door close.

"Divya, you were on TV for a few seconds. Jeez, the media is hyping this news up, aren't they?"

Roger's father opened the door again, enjoying the media attention.

"Yes, I think my son has flown the chariot. He is a remarkable young lad and is leading the team of children as we speak."

"Do you know what their agenda is? Why has no one else spotted them in any other part of the country until now?"

"All I can tell you now is that they are on a top-secret mission," said Jonathan, as if he knew what was going on.

Little did he know that he was right. The kids had not involved their parents, so Jonathan was not way off target.

His five minutes of fame spread throughout the country and penetrated the international frontiers, but not by much. Regardless of that, it was a major story on the domestic front.

It telecasted over several news channels in various Indian languages.

The Mistake

"Made in India, ek pyara soniya," was their ringtone. They were sitting in Pakistan and listening to the ringtone.

It was a song about a lovely girl (the singer), who was from India, and they further manufactured her heart in India.

"Whose phone is that?" It panicked Ram, because the sound was coming from close by, and the kids sometimes had the same ringtone as a show of unity. It can be the smallest of things that mean the most to some.

"It is your phone, Ram."

"They can track phones, Ram. Be careful."

Ram switched off the phone that instant. It was an unknown number; who else other than the police would be trying to call him?

The group was shocked. Did Ram not have the common sense to switch off his mobile phone?

"Sorry about this. The rest of you, please check if you have turned your phones off or not."

The children rummaged through their backpacks for their phones and found that they had all switched them off. It was Ram's alone that had been on.

The police smiled at the sheer genius of Mrs. Divya, Ram's mother. She had placed a beeping signal app in Ram's phone after the first instance when he and his gang ran away.

There was no way she would allow that situation to repeat itself and cause them to worry their heads off again. The thing was, she forgot that it was on his phone. All the hullabaloo about going to the police station, dodging reporters, etc., had driven that thought from her mind.

She alerted her friends and the police, once she remembered. The signal indicated that the children were somewhere in Pakistan.

"How the hell are they in Pakistan? Did you guys see them apply for a visa?"

It bewildered the police as much as it did the parents.

"The chariot."

Jonathan believed the story of flying chariots and country-hopping kids.

"Don't be ridiculous. No one can travel such a vast distance in under a day, and they don't have visas—and they don't have the money unless they have stolen from us, and that is not the case, here."

"And what do you think is happening here?" asked Jonathan, who did not enjoy being corrected as if he were a child.

Everyone stayed quiet. The press was just yards away and taking several photos of the parents, who had crowded into the small police station.

Ram did not know about the beeper app in his cell. He was crestfallen that he had made such a mistake. He could not bear to look at the others while walking.

Sheesha came to his rescue.

"Hey, Ram. Don't worry. Everyone makes mistakes." She rubbed his back. Ram did not get if she was trying to calm him down, or…? No one else was speaking to him, and though he felt grateful for the company, his senses warned him of something.

The tracer app did not work when switched off. He put away that thought in the back of his mind.

They carried on walking side by side, and Ram became a little uncomfortable. She was walking too close for comfort.

His mind sped away from the cell phone incident and was calculating the gap between them. He tried to keep a sizable distance without hurting her feelings.

Ram was a traditional guy and did not feel at ease whenever the opposite gender invaded his space.

It was getting dark, and Sheesha gave him a quick hug and a peck on his cheeks before scooting off, leaving a very confused and troubled Ram to his thoughts.

The mindset of Sheesha was thus:

-Things were happening to these children only.

-If things were to continue this way, they would leave her behind in some other quest of theirs.

So, she tried to become Ram's girlfriend, thinking that if the two of them were close, she would never be in want of adventure again.

It did not matter to her that she was older, but things unfolded differently than she expected.

"We wasted our time. We need to get back so we can sleep." Ram kept his voice low, but everyone heard him.

The kids turned toward the Wagah border, where their chariot was waiting for them.

"Lift the craft in the air."

"Why?"

"It is cooler up there and breezy. It is not like it is running on petrol or something like that. We will not add to global warming if that is what worries you."

"What if a plane hits us while we are sleeping?"

"This is a military-patrolled area. I think they will restrict its airspace. So, don't worry. I have not seen a single aircraft over here in this part of Pakistan since we first arrived, and so it's as safe as a Godrej bureau."

"Yeah. Okay, I got it."

"You didn't allow me to finish my sentence."

"I said, I got it, didn't I?"

The kids lifted the craft in the air, and within half an hour they fell into a deep sleep, fatigued from walking throughout the day. They had come close to dehydrating themselves.

"Ahem. Rise and shine, love birds."

Ram woke up to find Sheesha lying beside him wide awake and with full makeup on.

He turned around to see that the rest of the children were up and about. They were avoiding Ram and made no eye contact with him. Ram turned a lovely shade of pink. Thank God he was brown-skinned, and the color did not show much. Had he been fairer, perhaps, he would have glowed like a beacon.

Getting up, he managed a forced "Howdy, partner?" to no one in particular.

"I was just checking on you to see if everything was all right." Sheesha got up.

"Yeah, thank you. That is...um...kind of you." Ram's words did not ring true even in his ears, but Sheesha did not seem to notice.

"All right, let us set the bird down and find our way again."

They were making preparations to leave when, without warning, the Earth seemed to shake, and the tremor shook the floating chariot.

"What is that brilliant light?" yelled Rocky, but no one could hear him. They had gone deaf for a second.

That is when they realized that it was a bomb that had gone off, scaring the living daylights out of them.

Bloodied people were everywhere. Women screamed and children panicked. They ran without purpose like headless chicken, not knowing if their loved ones were alive or not.

"There is a stampede going on down there. What can we do?" Rocky's pupils were as wide as a crater on the moon. Again, his words fell on deaf ears.

Ram and Lakshmi gaped at the scene in utter shock.

The first thing that the children heard when they got back their hearing capacity was Sheesha screaming that they leave as soon as possible.

"I cannot be here. This is nuts. Let us get out of here."

"We need to help." Kumar voiced what Ram was thinking.

"Are you bonkers?" Spit was flying out of Roger's mouth as his eyes danced wildly, following the chaotic scene below. "We can't stay and help, you dunderhead." Then, seeing the rest looking at him in a disapproving manner, he added, "It is for our protection...my sister and all."

"He is right, Kumar. We are not the armed forces, trained to tackle terrorist activities. We better act our age for once and scoot."

"We can carry them out of here. We can—"

"There is not enough space for even us in this chariot. Where is the space for the rest of them?"

So, they decided to leave, and Kumar nodded along.

"Can we go to the site?"

"Helicopters are coming, Kumar. It is best we leave now."

There were gunshots fired, as it seemed the culprits were making a run for it.

"Do you want to stay any longer and maybe have popcorn as well?" sarcastic Sheesha cried in her shrill voice.

Within minutes, they had flown far away—so far away that all they could see around them were mountains and hills. The speed of the chariot was such that they couldn't gauge the distance they had covered in that short time.

"We need to know what the situation is like. We cannot be in the dark about what is going on."

"I have an idea." Ram opened his backpack and got the smartphone out.

"Is that the only way?" skeptical Lakshmi asked.

"Can you think of any other way?"

When Lakshmi remained silent, Ram turned on the news,

and the children huddled together.

"Breaking news," the reporter said. "There has been a bomb detonation in Pakistan, and the police are trying to bring order in the vicinity. People are paralyzed, and there is speculation that this may not be a one-time case. The police have shot the culprits, but they have not yet identified them."

"At least the perpetrators have been apprehended," Kumar murmured.

"Thirty-two dead, and they have injured an unknown number of people. They believe that the terrorists had planned on attacking the Wagha border, but it occurred prematurely. Authorities are still trying to put the pieces together. They've asked us to stay calm and collected."

Then they saw the police trying to chase the cameraman away from the spot.

"Have you heard of Lennon? I mean, John Lennon."

"What about him? I know that he was a singer of the previous generation or something like that."

"He said we do the act of love behind closed doors and that we exhibit hatred out in public. I think it sounds about right."

"The phone signal here is weak as a lamb. Please increase the volume of that news channel. I want to hear more."

"The United States has been the first country to condemn the act of terrorism, with the president promising to send help. India and Sri Lanka have also shown support in this terrible time, and the Indian prime minister has urged officials to take stringent actions to stop any more acts of terrorism from occurring."

"We must lie low for some time. This is not safe for us."

"What do you suggest that we do now?"

"Can you think of anywhere you would like to visit right now?"

"Get out of here?"

"Let us leave Pakistan for some time, and then when things settle down, we will come back."

"Our parents will watch us like hawks."

"That is why we are not going back home."

"We have little money to sustain ourselves."

"Then the obvious choice is Amritsar's Golden Temple."

"I hear that it is a peaceful place, but what is so special that we should want to go there?"

"The Punjabis are sympathetic people. They offer food in their temple at mealtimes for anyone and everyone."

"I have heard of this. What do they call these meals?"

"Langar," Ram and Lakshmi said together.

"This langar is available in any Sikh place of worship. Any particular reason we are going to Amritsar?"

"Don't you want to see the Golden Temple?"

"Okay, got it. Amritsar it is, then."

After flying to the Golden Temple, they found out they were too early for food.

"I am hungry."

"We have to wait. We can look around till that time."

The children roamed around till they came to Jallianwala Bagh.

"I have read about this place in history books. The Brits, when they ruled India, did not want meetings to be held. They were afraid of the freedom movement that was underway. They gave warning—"

"—and our brave freedom fighters would not listen."

"Yes, and so they came to this place where they heard a meeting was being conducted. They shot everyone. The Indians were unarmed. You can see their fingernail markings digging deep into the walls as the people tried to escape. The bullet marks are also there."

"There is a well somewhere here, right?"

"Yeah! Hordes of people jumped in, thinking they could hide. The sepoy just pointed their weapons down the well and shot till all were dead."

"Humans are so cruel."

"Tell me about it."

The brick walls surrounded them, and they felt a deep sense of sadness for the lost souls.

This was no way to die at all.

Now, the fun began:

The parents were catching a flight to Pakistan.

"What are the children up to? Why go to Pakistan?"

"There has been an explosive blast over there. I hope…"

"Let us not lose hope, honey. Be strong. They will be fine."

"No, they will not be," said Jonathan, who startled everyone. "I will wring their throats for sure this time."

"Shut up," John's father, Gregory, retorted. "That is a sure way to mislead children into thinking violence is the answer to all problems."

That is when the announcement came over the speakers: "May I have your attention, please? Flower Airlines regrets to announce the delay of its flight: FO 234 to Karachi. We request passengers to stand by for further announcements. Thank you."

"Oh, no." Ram's mom lost her cool.

"We have to leave now. Do you understand that? Do you even have children? Do you, huh?"

"Madam, there is a technical problem. Our engineers are working on it, and we should be able to resolve the issue soon. We are sorry for the inconvenience caused." The duty manager tried to keep a neutral expression, but the shouting had made people turn and stare.

"You have not answered my question yet. Do you or do you not have children of your own?"

"Please, can we can go to my cabin and discuss this there?"

"I don't want to go there. I just want my children back, and that can happen only when the flight leaves."

The duty manager was at a loss for what to say, but the other parents came to the rescue and escorted her back to the waiting area.

The crowd that had gathered to watch this scene with the duty manager dispersed.

A few minutes later, the manager came back with a cup of mango juice to calm the disturbed mother, and with a warm smile, handed it to her.

Everyone appreciated the gesture and thanked her.

After the hour was up, the manager made sure that the group of parents were the first to board the aircraft.

Back to the children:

"I think it is time to go back and resume our search."

"So, where do we go now?"

"We cannot go to the Wagha border, as it may be like Fort Knox there."

"Then where?"

"It should have been the first thing we did."

"What are you saying, Ram?"

"We fly to the place marked on the map."

"Ha, ha. Yeah, that makes more sense."

The Book of Power

The children flew on the silent vimana. Watching the birds fly by, they marveled at God's creative prowess.

They took a little time to search for the place. When they got there, they found out it was an outdated and abandoned home.

"Why would the map point to this shack? What do you see as significant about this place?"

"Why do you think there should be something significant to this place?"

"Why else would some old and powerful secret society hide it here?"

The children made their way up the stairs of the house and combed through it.

"There is nothing here. Maybe it was just a joke that someone played on us. Maybe the map is wrong."

"Look around you, Kumar. We have come here on a flying chariot. Nothing that seemed to be true is right anymore."

"We'll go down to the basement and check. Why don't you guys check the ground floor?" Ram did not wait for a reply, and he didn't get one. His companions typically followed and trusted him, but this time, Roger spoke up.

"As you said before, this is serious business. People have hidden it for a good reason. We cannot expect every book to be in plain sight. I do not think it wise to split up right now. The rest I leave to your good judgment."

There was a minute's pause while Ram contemplated.

"You're right. We must stick together."

They spread out and searched the ground floor. After turning up nothing of interest, they proceeded to the basement.

"It is dark and dirty here."

"Did you expect the beach winds to blow through your hair gently?"

The kids laughed, but as the staircase led deep into the darkness, they became quiet.

"I don't like it. I feel something is wrong."

"Keep quiet," whispered Leela. "Can you not see that the others are already feeling like they will meet the big bad wolf?"

"Sorry about that."

"Did you bring anything to light the way, or can you see a light switch?"

"I smell gasoline."

They found a wooden stick wrapped up in a cloth dipped in gasoline.

"There is a cigarette lighter here," Roger offered.

"Do you smoke?"

"Yeah, so what?"

"Nothing."

Lighting the stick, they looked around the basement.

Gautham jumped, which nearly gave the others a heart attack.

"What are you doing?"

"Can you hear the hollow sound? There's something here. Maybe a loose floorboard."

Tap, tap, tap. "Yeah! Sure, it is loose," replied Rocky, startled.

"Leela, your eyes are popping out of your sockets."

"I did not realize that you could see so well in this dim light."

"Guys, guys."

"Wonder where it leads to?"

"I need to quote a line from a movie." Rocky paused for effect, then said, "There is only one way to find out."

The kids, half-cautious and half-terrified, lifted the loose floorboard and entered the secret passage one by one.

Much to their amazement, they ended up in a cute little room. It was light-pink in color, like a child had painted it. The floor had a picture of the sign of the book of power. A circular patch with an intricate design of triangles and rhombuses. Strange markings made it stand out. The problem was the cobwebs hanging above.

"Hey, there are rotten supplies over here. It must be a good find for an archaeologist."

"Ew. That is a human skull." Lakshmi was taken aback.

"What is so 'ew' about it? You and I have one too." Rocky teased fiercely. He was scared and his voice was high-pitched.

"This room leads to many places." There were passages going deep into the Earth. Rocky peered curiously at the entrances. *Where are we supposed to go?* He wondered. *Which passage is right?*

"I see a switch here," Ram exclaimed.

"Isn't that too modern? Do you think electricity runs through here? Who pays the bill?" Lakshmi was curious.

"Do we care?" Rocky had heard enough.

"Turn it on, and let's see what happens." Lakshmi ordered.

"Here goes nothing." Ram switched it on.

The passage filled with light, blinding the children for a moment. They shaded their eyes with their hands. But only one of the passages lit up. The others stayed dark.

That decides that, Rocky smiled.

The deeper they explored, the scarier it got. The imagination can run wild in this type of setting, even if there is no reason to worry. Ali was biting his fingernails.

"You, over there. Can you see it?" Kumar pointed.

"There is a huge hole in the floor," gasped Leela.

"Oh, my God." Lakshmi drew her breath in. What kind of a nightmare was this?

"There are spikes down in the pit." Rocky's shaky voice echoed through the cave.

When they came closer to the huge gap in the floor, they stopped and had a look. The floor had huge, sharp needles tall enough to kill a small elephant.

"We must find a way across. We cannot go back now—we have come so far. The book is just across the pit, waiting for us."

Everyone looked crestfallen—everyone except Kumar, that is.

"Don't...," Kumar raised his voice, "... concentrate on the problem at hand. Look beyond." He pointed. "Look above you."

"Are those rings?"

"Are we expected to hang onto those and swing from one to another? That is madness. I don't think I can. I will fall, and we all know what that means."

"We must try." Ram was taking the driver's seat again. "Thank you, Kumar. I will go first."

"Ram, be careful. This is a booby trap. What if one ring falls off because time has decayed it?" The idea clearly petrified Leela.

"We are doing this for our friend, and if friendship does not matter when you need it most, then it is not friendship."

"The rings are too high. How are we to reach them? Even the tallest of us cannot reach one of them. I don't think any person could, even if they were adults or teens."

"I see a camouflaged ladder stuck to the wall. We can climb that and see what happens."

Ram started first, and it led to a ledge from where the rings were accessible. He gripped the first one and gave it a tug. It did not fall off.

"Steady, Ram."

As soon as he swung, the roof moved, descending downward. It was a steady and slow descent, giving a respectable time to make it. The distance to cover was horribly long. The girls did not know how they would cross the chasm.

"If you don't get to the other end before it comes down, it will squash you on the spikes. Be careful."

The children watched with bated breath as Ram made his way from one ring to another like a monkey.

Ram made it across with some time to spare. All the kids clapped hard, and it sounded as though the Earth itself was clapping for him. The echo was so loud down there.

The roof with the rings attached made its course back to where it belonged, rising a little faster than it had come down.

"I cannot do this. It is way too hard and risky."

Kumar paid no heed to their comments and made his way up the ladder.

"So, the next act in this circus show begins."

"Shut up, Roger. No one asked for your input here."

Kumar was on the ledge now, but he wasn't sure what to do next. Ali, who was looking around for other options, saw a hanky sticking out of Kumar's pocket.

"I have a brilliant idea," he exclaimed. Kumar came down from the ledge, and Ali explained the plan. Kumar broke a huge chunk of Earth from the wall—to everyone's amazement—then climbed back up to the ledge.

"Do you want to dig your way across, man? We will be fossils by the time we reach the other end—or worse, it will crush us when this place caves in, thanks to you."

Kumar took out his hanky and placed dirt inside it. It was pearly white, and he tied the loose knots together so it could hold the soil.

The roof now slid back in its place; Kumar tied it to the first ring. Again, the roof slid down because it was as sensitive to the weight as a touch-me-not plant.

Kumar jumped onto the roof and walked to the other end, where Ram beamed with pride. What they did not see at the beginning was that the roof was not a roof at all. It was a platform—a false ceiling.

"Hello, Ram." Kumar smiled. "Smart of these guys, creating a deception to hide the real purpose of the platform. People don't think there could be space to walk on it rather than to hang from it. Do you get me?" Kumar was rambling.

The claps were again thunderous, and one by one they walked across.

"Never leave home without a hanky," Kumar mimicked his mother, and everyone laughed. It broke the tension.

The others had begun walking across the platform when it suddenly rose again. It paralyzed them for a second with fear, and then they ran, screaming.

"Gautham, hurry."

But Gautham had tripped and was the last one on the platform. If it continued to rise, he would not be able to jump from such a height, and if he didn't, he would be chutney.

Ram jumped up and caught the railing. The roof again descended. Gautham jumped off. The children, alarmed for Ram, yelled. His feet and torso had already sunk into the pit.

"Let go of the railing, Ram, and grab my hand." Kumar was on all fours, trying to keep his brain calm.

Ram did as Kumar had instructed. There was no need for his friend to tell him twice.

The roof halted and forced its way back to the ceiling.

They all helped pull a sweaty Ram up. It was time for a group hug, and they huddled together.

"Keep moving," Gautham thundered to no one in particular. He needed to walk this thing off. The more he stood, the more he could not stand it. His nerves were on end.

"What is that awful stench? I feel like throwing up on the floor." Lakshmi was green in the face.

"Keep away from me, then. I smell nothing." Ali moved away quickly. But it was not long before the stench caught up to everyone's noses.

Leela vomited.

"The sewage line for the entire city is flowing through here. Someone has to cross it, though." Ali calculated their chances. It did not look good.

"Someone? Who?" Roger was concerned they might ask him to do it.

"Shall we do 'Inky, Pinky, Ponky' for this and decide who we should send?" Ali joked. It was not the right time.

"I cannot let this go on," said Ram, and for a second, Leela was not sure if she had heard him.

"We came all this way, and now you want us to turn back? Is that all Gopal means to you?" Leela said in a forced composed voice.

"Gopal means a lot, but I cannot risk someone going into the sewage. It is full of feces, and anyone who gets stuck in it will drown for sure. It is not like you can swim over here. You understand that this is not safe at all. The risk of losing a life is high in this case."

"I don't want your lecture." Leela looked as though nothing would stop her from getting that book, and if it meant that she had to die to get it, she would. That worried Ram for many reasons. She was crying and could not stop shaking.

"There," said Gautham. "The book is lying over there. There are no booby traps." Ram looked to see where Gautham was pointing. It looked like a small podium on which the book lay. The book was thinner than the one they carried on them.

Yet the markings and the design looked identical. A cover design worth looking at, the book appeared to be solid and magical.

"What if there is one right in the midst of this drainage? We cannot cross here." Ram turned back.

Leela tried jumping in, but Ram pulled her back. She tried wriggling away, but his hold was like iron.

"You are manhandling a woman," she shouted.

"I am not yet a man, and you are not yet a woman either. We are what adults call kids."

"Leave me alone. I will get the book of power."

"We can do this together."

"I thought you would not come?" Leela stopped squirming.

"Look behind you. There is a passage there hidden from our eyes while coming this way but in plain sight when we look back from this angle."

"What does it say on the top?"

"'Know when to quit and when to pursue.' Had you jumped in, you would have died."

Leela stopped struggling.

It was a small passage built into the rocks that circumvented the issue at hand.

At last, they reached the book of power. It felt light, just as Roger expected it to be. The pages were smooth and deceptively simple to look at. It hid the fact that the knowledge contained within could make or break nations.

"Does anyone think it weird that the message we got said eight will find what the nine left behind, but there are ten of us here?"

"All people make mistakes. Leave it. We have new things to worry about right now."

"It is lunchtime," Rocky said.

"Only you can think of food when we are so close to sewage."

The others laughed, but Leela swooned and fainted.

The Secret of the Swollen Girl

"She looks pale. I wonder what is amiss with her?" But now Ram was getting an idea of what was taking place, and he was not sure how to react to that thought.

"I and Kumar..."

"It should be: Kumar and I," corrected Sheesha, thinking she was the only one who knew how to use the English language.

"Okay...um...Kumar and I will hold Leela's legs, and you two...," he pointed at Rocky and Roger, "...hold her shoulders, and we can carry her out."

"She's heavy," puffed Roger.

"You are just like a possum," teased a struggling Rocky. "What has this girl eaten to be so beefed up?" His face became red with the effort to carry her.

"Careful now," warned a grim-looking Ram. "She is not well, and if you aren't careful, I swear to God, I will punch a hole through your thick skulls."

"No need for such strong language."

Still, Ram looked so dangerous that the others were unwilling to test him on his words.

"Where there is sewage, there are rats," said Lakshmi, eyeing something at the far end. "And I don't see the rats," she whimpered.

"Is that not a good thing?" Leela was confused.

Lakshmi said, "Not if the snakes that hunt it look hungry, and we are the only ones around. They must have run out of their food."

"They would have starved to death, wouldn't they?" Rocky tried to solve the issue with one simple statement.

"This is a magical place, and they are meant as a guard. They were not here when we came. They are here to stop us from leaving." Ali voiced Lakshmi's thoughts.

"Run." Ram had nothing better to say.

They took out their smartphones and flashed lights right into the eyes of a number of serpents as they made their way across, but one fell on Sheesha.

"Aaagh!"

A banshee would have been proud of that scream.

The terrified snake was shaken free and slithered away.

"Good one. You proved that you are scarier than a snake in a dark pit." Lakshmi was unsympathetic.

They came across a snakeskin.

"You scared the skin out of that snake, Sheesha. Here it is," Rocky teased.

The children laughed.

"Roof's up, and there are no ladders I can see on this side. How are we leaving?" Ali was becoming chatty.

"Snakes," Leela said weakly.

"What about them?" Sheesha was cheesed off.

"How did they find a way into this place? There must be another entrance, because we did not see them until we came here," Leela explained, her energy draining more with every second.

"Good idea, but the holes might be too small for us to crawl through." Ali saw a hole in the theory.

"It was just an idea. I don't think we can go out through the sewage line, because the sign said if you jump in, then you will die," Lakshmi reminded the lot.

"I will never see sunlight again and have the wind rustle my hair as we fly across in the chariot," Kumar said, then took out his flute and played a sad song.

There was pin-drop silence as they listened to the song, and then Ram jumped up.

"Did a snake bite you?" Lakshmi's head shot right up.

"Well, no." For a second Ram looked confused. "I had an idea. If a horse can fly and a chariot can fly, then why cannot we? We can use the book of power to cast a spell on ourselves and use it to fly across this stupid pit."

So, they tried. As usual, Ram was the first to test out his idea, and once he flew across, the others followed suit.

"I am so weary. This flying business is tiresome." The chubby boy, Rocky, looked like he had just been hauling around a Herculean burden. He and Roger had carried Leela across.

"We flew across the pit, and we got our energy sapped out of us...." Ali was analytical.

"A horse has more stamina and is stronger than a bunch of kids," Ram continued.

"Back to the chariot, it is." Lakshmi was resigned to the idea.

What they didn't realize was that Leela lost her phone back at the old and abandoned house. It was lost for good.

"We need to get back to India so we can get Leela to a hospital." Roger was in no mood to let another friend die in front of him. Not if he could help it.

"We cannot waste any time. I wonder what is wrong with her?" Sheesha's comment brought them back to the issue at hand.

"The adventure must have been too much for her." Lakshmi piped up. She did not make eye contact with anyone. She hoped they would leave the subject and not drill her for more information.

"How weak," Sheesha said with a scorn on her face.

Lakshmi seethed. She was close to slapping the egotistical girl.

The chariot flew on, and the fresh air made things better for Leela. Her sweaty face was clearing up, and her breathing became more regular. Her eyes fluttered open, but she stayed where she was and did not try to move.

They landed on the Indian side of Punjab and took her to a hospital.

"What do we do for money?"

"We take her to G.H."

"General hospital?"

"Or government hospital... I don't know."

"They don't ask for money?"

"No, they do it for free—for a small thing like sweating and stuff."

"She could be in a grave state. Only a doctor can say how severe it is."

They ran to the receptionist, who looked a little harassed by the crowd of people that thronged the area.

"Excuse me."

The receptionist looked down and seemed relieved that she was talking to kids and not angry adults. "How can I help you guys?"

"My friend fainted, and we have no money."

"Please sit in the waiting area, and we will call you."

"But this could be severe and life-threatening. Can't you take her to the ICU now?"

"There is no need for the ICU. She is dehydrated. Give her some water. There is drinking water in the corner."

The kids helped Leela to a chair and fetched water for her.

"How long do you think we have to wait?"

"Depends."

"On what?"

"Since they will do this for free, there will be a huge crowd lining up, and we may not get a chance till later."

"I will feed them a rat's tail if they make us wait for over ten minutes."

"Good luck with that. No, you are inspirational." The sarcasm was clear.

"Wait here." Rocky walked to the nearest member of the medical personnel he could find and said, "Doctor, my friend fainted and needs care. Can you help us?"

"I am a nurse and not a doctor. Show me your friend, and I will see if I can help her. But make it quick. I need to get back and cannot keep the doctor waiting for long."

Rocky led the way to where Leela was sitting, but she had already gotten up.

"Thank you, Mr. Balbir Singh." Leela saw the nametag on the nurse's chest. "But I am feeling better. I am just hungry. That is all."

"Ah, I thought so. There is a canteen down there, and they do not charge for food for kids and women, as per our hospital policy. Help yourselves."

There was a huge crowd shuffling around downstairs, and the kids had to wait their turn to get food.

Leela attacked her ration and gobbled up enough to feed two people. The kids watched in amazement.

***

"It is very nice of the Pakistan government to issue us a visa on a priority basis. I am not sure they believed our story, but thank God we had their mobile numbers to point out they were there somewhere. We have again lost the signal on Ram's cell, and so the Pakistan police cannot find them, but I believe that even they have a lot on their plate at the moment."

"We will have to find them ourselves. That's a given."

"I cannot wait for this plane to land. We need to find them. It has been days since they left."

After a long wait, the plane touched the ground, and the parents flooded out. They headed straight to the foreign exchange to get the Pakistani currency.

"Not much difference in value. They take the amount for the service they provide. It is like giving these people free money. We gain nothing."

"Can you focus on the matter at hand?"

"Oh, yeah! I forgot."

"How could you forget? They are our children."

"I know, woman. You don't have to tell me."

"Speak with respect. You learn to speak with respect first."

"Look who's talking."

Divya put her two fingers under her tongue and whistled out loud. That got the people in the vicinity, including the group of parents she had accompanied, to turn around. "I cannot believe that you are all bickering like children. We need to be more mature. Our kids seem to have more sense than us, since they did all this and more when they landed here."

The group walked in silence. Divya noticed the sounds of a security dog sniffing the people waiting in line for security checks as she left the airport.

That night, everyone except Jonathan went to bed early. He stayed back in the bar and drank like a fish. That night, there was a semi-celebrity performing in that hotel and a few reporters in attendance.

"You don't know nothing," slurred Jonathan, looking at the lovely reporter who was taking a rest at the bar.

She ignored him.

"I said, you don't know nothing. Did you hear me?" Jonathan walked over to her.

She looked up at him with cold eyes. "I think you meant: I don't know anything. Now, please, leave me alone."

"I have the story of a lifetime: ten kids flying to Pakistan without visas."

That grabbed her attention.

"Sir, you are drunk. Maybe you're mistaken?" She was cautious.

"You can check it out with the registry in this hotel. There are twenty parents here in one group from India."

"So, you are from India?" She licked her lips in anticipation. It was an unconscious move.

"Haven't you been listening, woman?" Jonathan was talking to her nose.

"Pray, continue." She hid her irritation well.

"We are here for our kids, whom we tracked down. They don't have jurisdiction here, so we came ourselves."

"You are talking about Indian police?" She was recording the conversation.

"Woman, have you lost your marbles? Can the Pakistan police lose jurisdiction in Pakistan? It is the Indian police who lost the juris...ris...juris...diction." He hiccupped.

Then, he poured out the story. That same night, the press released the news.

The morning paper read: "My children have no passport, but they came to Pakistan."

It caused quite a stir, and when the parents woke up, the press was waiting.

"Not again. How did the press sniff this out so fast?"

"I guess that the media people are super-fast here." Jonathan burped. "Ah, my head... It hurts as though someone whacked it with a cricket bat."

"Were you drunk last night?"

"What? It upsets me to lose my children."

"And you blurted our story out to a reporter?"

"She was cunning and took it out of my mouth."

"You idiot."

Mrs. Niketan walked in. "You must see this." She increased the volume on the TV.

Photos of the ten children flashed across the screen, and the reporter covering the story was speaking in Urdu.

"Do any of you know Urdu?"

"No."

"Then please turn on an English news channel."

"Um...okay."

The TV came alive with a female's high-pitched tone.

"I believe ten children have come into Pakistan without legal permits. These immigrants have somehow escaped detection, and the debate for tonight is: Do you see it from the parents' point of view or from the law's point of view? Should a punishment be handed out to the children, or should they release them into the custody of the family members?"

Mrs. Niketan turned the TV off.

"You fool!" She looked at Jonathan in utter disbelief at what he had done. "You are turning into a real nuisance for us," she added, not knowing that their children were no longer in Pakistan.

They left the hotel via the back entrance and found themselves on a small crooked street that smelled of chicken feathers.

"At least we made it out." Jonathan gave an artificial laugh.

"Why did we bring that buffoon along?" whispered Divya to Mrs. Niketan.

No one liked illegal immigrants, that was for sure. There had been a call for justice following the bomb's blast, and security forces had to swallow the anger of the mob. Then, this had happened; the Pakistanis could not take it anymore.

"The hotel van is there."

The van took them two streets from the hotel, and then the battery died, embarrassing the driver.

"My apologies. I am sorry, but I cannot take you any further. It will take time."

"We cannot wait. We will find our own way, thanks."

They got out of the van.

"Look, it's the people from the news."

"I heard that your children are here without permits."

"Get out of our country, you illegal immigrants."

"Now, wait a sec. We have a visa."

But the crowd was not listening. They took up stones and pelted the parents, who ran. The crowd followed behind them.

"What are you doing?" panted Mrs. Niketan.

"Reading the horoscope." With deep breaths Jonathan was holding on to today's newspaper, which he had taken from the hotel. "I want to see if I will survive today."

"Jonathan, you will not survive unless you drop that paper and run faster."

The street dogs barked. Mrs. Niketan, who was a slow runner, was zigzagging in order to avoid the dogs. It would have been funny had it not been for the seriousness of the situation.

The saree she was wearing made her run slower than usual, and she was puffing. Her stamina seemed to be running out.

The other ladies removed their shoes to pick up speed.

"There are twenty of us. Maybe we should turn and fight. We are like a mob ourselves."

"Half of them are women. How can we fight?"

"Maybe we can throw stones, or something?"

"Run, man, and stop yapping."

They were running downhill. Out of nowhere, a group of children appeared on their bicycles.

"Here, Uncle. Take our cycles. That will be better for you."

"Thank you so much, kiddo. Allah bless you."

The children beamed with delight at hearing that.

"There are not enough cycles for all of us. We have to squeeze three onto one bike."

The group, along with the poor winded Mrs. Niketan, rolled down the sloping road and left their pursuers behind.

Unfortunately for the parents, the road soon sloped upward again.

"We cannot ride the bikes up the slope. We need to ditch them."

So, they ran again, and the mob continued running after them.

In all the confusion, more media people rolled in with their news vans.

"Can't these guys help us out?"

"Why? They are getting the story of their lifetime."

"It may not help us, but thank God that they aren't hindering us, either. Why are they behaving like they are on a safari watching animals? They are acting like spectators in an open-air theater."

"The freaking people are just rolling their cameras and flashing lights at us. I wish I had the time to pick up a stone and—"

"Okay. That is enough."

The parents were just across the street from the old house that the children had been to.

"Is this not the place where we got the last signal? Maybe the children are here somewhere?"

A man from the mob named Imran called the police.

"The parents are here."

"Parents?"

"Those kids from the TV who have no visa. Their parents are—"

"Sir, the parents have visas. There is nothing the police can do, but if you are pursuing them, then we will come and sort things out."

Imran hung up the phone, but not before the police had traced the call.

The mob was comprised of a number of old people, who were also running out of breath. They threw stones, and some with cigar lighters tore cloth and lit it. They then rolled it onto a rock and threw it at the running parents.

Divya screamed more with anger than in fear.

"Bananas for sale," yelled a vendor.

Divya picked up a few and hurled one at the angry mob. It hit Imran in the face and made him lose his balance.

Divya's phone rang.

"Hello," she panted.

"Mom."

"Ram?"

"Yeah."

"Where in God's name are you?"

Ram lied, "I am in Valluvar Kottam," knowing full well he was in Amritsar.

"We are in Pakistan."

Ram thought he had not heard her well through the terrible phone line connection.

"What are you doing there?" he asked with false innocence.

"Stay in Valluvar Kottam, or go home, and we will be there in a few days' time. All the parents are here in Pakistan searching for you guys."

They came to a cul-de-sac.

"Mother of God! We are done for."

"Have hope."

Mrs. Niketan cried.

Gregory, John's father, knocked on a gate that seemed locked.

An old man came scurrying up after noticing the situation and opened the gate. The parents rushed in and found that they were in a mosque.

"We cannot hurt them here," muttered Imran under his breath. "What are we going to do?"

"We can do nothing but leave."

"I want to sit awhile and pray by myself, so I'm going to the mosque."

The religious leader was Aaban Shah, and he took the parents to the airport in his bus. The parents did not know if they could get a flight back the very same day.

"Thank you, sir."

"It was Allah's will you came to our mosque and saw the serene environment there."

"We can't thank you enough."

"It was Allah's will" was all he said as he turned away.

"What are we going to do with our luggage?"

"The impression I got from Ram is that the children are back in Chennai, or they never left. But, why he didn't call for so long is something beyond my understanding."

"And how did we track them to Pakistan? Was there some kind of technical glitch? They couldn't have been to Pakistan, right?"

"I am confused myself."

"What the...?" A pigeon took a dump on Mrs. Lalitha's head. She wiped it off with a hanky she always carried—the same type she had always asked Kumar to take, which ended up saving the kids a lot of trouble.

"I am off to the whiskey shop. The duty-free goods will be the best thing to have happened on this trip, since I can't find my son to flog him."

Jonathan's behavior shocked the other parents.

"Excuse me, sir! How many stops does this flight have to make before reaching Chennai?"

"The flight is nineteen hours," The ticket counter staff member replied like a parrot who had not been listening to a word of what had been asked. He then moved on to the next customer.

"Bozo," she muttered under her breath.

Divya called her son. "Ram, we will be there soon, and I have not given the keys to the neighbors. We got tickets to Chennai because it is a weekday. Bide your time, and then I will see you, okay? Are the others doing well, and are they with you?"

"Yeah, Mom. Everyone's here, and they are all fine."

Ram repeated his conversation with his mother to the other kids.

"Then we have time to kill."

"Don't you want to find out how to use this book?"

"That can wait. We will have enough *time* later on, anyway." He winked.

"We can explore the north before going back."

"Where do you want to go? Jammu and Kashmir, Leh...?"

"Kasauli."

"Where is that? I have never heard of that place."

"It is close to Chandigarh and is not open for high commercial traffic. So, it is stunning. It is in Himachal Pradesh."

"Okay, upward and onward to Kasauli."

"It is so close to Shimla."

They breathed in the fresh air and relaxed at the highest point on the mountain.

"There is no one here. It is so peaceful. I did not know that there was a part of India where there is no one about. This is radical."

"Where did you learn that word: radical?"

"Cartoons, baby. I never stopped watching them."

They parked their vimana and lay on the cool green grass.

"Aah, this is the life. I can get used to this."

Ram was sitting a little further away and closer to the edge.

"Hi, Ram."

"Hey, Sheesha." Ram braced himself and forgot to breathe.

"Can I ask you some candid questions?"

"Would you not ask, if I say no?"

"Not really."

"Then...?"

"Do you have a girlfriend?"

Ram's worst fears were getting confirmed.

"Um...not interested in having one yet. I will, once I get a little older. Excuse me, let me check on the others."

"You can run, but you can't hide," she whispered to herself.

Roger was not far off, and he heard everything, quickly filling with the protective feeling that every sibling gets.

"If Ram does not behave with proper etiquette toward my sister...," he mumbled.

Roger was too narrow-minded, which was what Sheesha was counting on.

"Ram," Sheesha called, and Ram turned around. "My birthday is coming up, and I wanted to invite you as a special guest to the party."

Everyone turned to look at Ram, who had gone a tad bit pink. She was too forward, and Ram did not like it one bit—though he felt flattered.

"We will all be there," he responded, trying to evade the actual question. Sheesha did not pursue, and Ram thanked all the Gods from all religions for saving him.

Roger was getting angrier. Ram's disinterest had planted the seed of hatred in his heart, and it seemed to be nurtured well by Sheesha. She knew how to water the plant.

"Ram is avoiding me."

"That rascal."

"Roger, I feel so sad and used by him," she said with a sorrowful expression. It was an act, but Roger fell for it.

"I will kill him."

"We can do better."

"What do you mean?"

"This is the plan..." And she whispered something into Roger's ear.

"I like it. We won't allow them to revive Gopal. Simple as that."

"Try catching this." Ali threw a round stone as high as he could.

"Watch the great one in action and learn from a pro." Gautham did not take his eyes off the stone and caught it. "It is a little hard on the hands."

"My turn to catch. Do your worst."

Leela got up and walked over to Ram. "I want to talk to my parents. Can I have the phone, please?"

Kumar, who always had his flute with him, played a catchy tune. Lakshmi and Sheesha listened. Roger and Ram joined the gang and applauded his fine playing abilities.

"After all this is over, maybe we can go to Maldives, or Thailand, or someplace nice."

The children then walked to monkey point. Legend has it that while returning from the Himalayas carrying the "Sanjeevani plant," Lord Hanuman had touched this mountain with his foot, and that is why the place is foot-shaped. They could see Chandigarh from there.

"What is that over there?"

"I think it is an air force base."

"That is like Christmas has come early."

A fighter jet whizzed past their head.

"Yahoo."

For a full fifteen minutes, they watched the death-defying stunts performed by the jets overhead.

"Amazing. Maybe we can do the same with our chariot?"

"That would be terrifying."

"Life is for taking risks."

"Life is not for acting dumb."

"I think they are practicing for the annual air show."

"Annual shows means they hold it every year. Do you think they will perform the annual show twice per year, or something?"

"Thank you, professor," Rocky said sullenly.

"What is that trailing behind the crafts?"

Squinting his eyes, Rocky read: "VICTORY IS OURS."

Wham!

Two of the planes crashed into each other in mid-air. The sound of iron crunching was deafening as they hit Earth.

One pilot had pressed the ejection button, while the other pilot never made it out of his craft before it hit the ground.

"He will not make it, Ram," Kumar called when he saw that Ram had rushed to the pilot's aid.

"There is the smell of gas. Get away from there before it explodes."

Ram was not listening.

"Hello? Are you okay? Are any of your bones broken, or

something? Can I pull you out?"

"Whether my bones are in bits and pieces or not, I need to get away from this craft as fast as possible. Can you help me out, please?"

Ram opened the door and pulled the pilot out of the cockpit.

"Aaah." The pilot let out a groan as he saw his twisted ankle.

Ram put his arm around the pilot and steadied him. Kumar and Rocky rushed to his aid.

Boom!

The plane exploded, and it threw them forward. Shards of glass pierced the surrounding earth, and one fell harmlessly on Kumar.

"Are you all right, Kumar?"

"I am feeling peachy."

"Good. Now help him to his feet and let's get away as fast as possible."

The girls rushed over. "Are you bonkers? Have you lost your marbles? What were you thinking?"

"The girls are right, boy. You could have got yourself in deep trouble had it been a minute later. I thank you for saving me, but it was foolhardy of you." The pilot looked at Kumar and Rocky. "All of you."

"We saved your life, and you are complaining?"

"Not complaining, my friend. I feel like running around you guys like a puppy happy to see its master. It was the thought of your safety before you considered this aged man. You guys still have to live your life. I am just saying this out of concern."

"Thanks." Ram did not know what else to say.

"Can you guys escort me to the base?"

So, the kids walked, and the pilot hobbled all the way to the air force base.

"Have you guys eaten lunch yet?"

"No." Rocky overreacted when he heard those magic words.

"Would you like to join me in the officer's mess for some food? I assure you that the food is excellent."

Before anybody else could answer, Rocky said, "No. No. Yes."

"What does that mean?"

"My mother asked me to refuse the first two times and accept the third time only, and so it is: No. No. Yes."

"Ha, ha. Okay. You guys go to the mess hall and eat while I will report to my supervisor. He will not like it."

"Also, go to the medical department and get your leg fixed before coming."

It took time for the pilot to return.

"I am going back to the chariot to rest."

"I will also come with you, Leela." Sheesha slipped into the shoes she had removed to cool her feet.

When at long last the pilot returned, the kids were sleepy because of the cold mountain air.

"Do you guys want to take a refreshing swim?"

"Is there a swimming pool here?"

"There is, but I was not talking about the pool. I was talking about a river nearby called Kaushalya. It is pretty soothing and has herbs that make the water medicinal."

"There are no sharks in it, right?" Kumar was biting his nails again.

"Ha, ha. No there aren't any, but perhaps a few crocodiles." When he saw the expression on the children's faces, he said, "I was just joking. It is safe."

"How about the current?"

"Not too much."

"The depth?"

"Not too much either. All clear now?"

"Okay, let's go."

After a fifteen-minute ride along a road that wound around like the intestines in their stomachs, they reached their destination.

The children jumped into the pool with their clothes on. That was one way to wash clothes and take a bath. It seemed like a long time since their previous one. Everyone was smelly.

"Officer, why don't you join us as well?" Roger seemed too courteous.

First, he was hesitant, but eventually the officer also joined them.

Roger, quick as a rat, got out of the river and drove off in the car, his leg barely able to press the accelerator.

"The book. He has the book."

"What book?" inquired the officer, but the children did not reply.

Roger did not know how to drive and banged into many things.

"Get out of the way. I don't know which of the three pedals is the break." He was racing to the top of the mountain.

Was he daydreaming about the book of power while driving? Was that the reason he did not see the old man on the street? The vehicle hit him, but not with full force, otherwise the man would have succumbed to his injuries.

Roger got out of the car and ran. The old man's son, who was with him when the incident happened, ran after the boy.

Roger was a marathon runner, but the thin mountain air didn't provide a lot of oxygen. The boy in pursuit was more familiar with the conditions, but he was not a runner. So, it was an evenly matched race, with neither gaining nor losing ground.

"Come here, you rat." A punch from nowhere hit Roger. Roger fell but was quick to get back up and had a stone ready in his hand. He hit the other boy in the head with it, who fainted.

Leela saw the boys' scuffle and knew something was wrong. Where were the others, and why was Roger hitting a stranger with a stone?

Before she could get her answers, Sheesha overpowered her, who then tied up and gagged her.

Sheesha had stayed back in the pretense of helping. She now banded with Roger to take Leela as a captive. They had her on the chariot as they flew away.

By now the children had reached the place of the accident. The furious officer got the car and took it back to his base.

"We must reach the top. Leela and Sheesha are there. I don't know who is in trouble. Leela, I think."

"There," Rocky exclaimed. "There is a lad on the ground."

"Help him up."

"Aaah. My head."

"What happened?"

"That stupid boy hit me with a stone."

"What did you do to him?"

"Nothing! He smashed into my father, and I chased him. Was he your friend?"

"He double-crossed us."

"Serves you right for having such a character as your friend."

"Hey, be nice. Did you see any girls?"

"I was fighting, so I was not looking anywhere else."

"I can't believe that Leela was also in on it." Ram spat on

the ground.

"Ram, you cannot doubt her."

"She is not on our side. If she was, she would also be lying on the ground unconscious."

"You cannot question her loyalty. She wants to revive Gopal more than anyone else."

"How can you be so sure?"

Lakshmi took a deep breath. "She is growing fatter, right?"

"So what?"

"Ever wonder why she is pale and yet growing fat?"

Ram had wondered before. Now his worst fears seemed to be coming true.

"She is pregnant, isn't she? Who is the father?"

"Gopal." There was a ringing silence. "It was a mistake, that was all."

"Pregnancy can make you cry, vomit, have mood swings, and all those things. Be empathetic."

The Last Hurrah

The children sat on the grass and waited for a miracle to happen. Their parents would be home soon, and the children would not be there. This time, they were in for some serious punishment.

"God does not help those who cannot help themselves."

"Thanks for that useful tip."

"You are welcome."

"I will kill you."

"Not if I get you first."

"Shut up."

"You shut up."

"We have no money, and we are in a foreign place—though in India. We do not understand how to speak the local language. We can't ask our parents for help nor go to the police to answer awkward questions."

"We get the point. Life screwed us."

The older boy, who Roger had hit, pitied them and took them to his home.

"My name is Jitender, and I would love to know your names, but I will forget them again, and so no point in asking. You guys can crash here for the night."

"How is your father doing?"

"It was more of a shock than anything else. The impact was not all that bad, and so he escaped with just a few bruises.

How come you guys are here all alone?"

"School outing, but we got lost."

The children tried to hide their smiles.

"I can't go to the market tomorrow because I have to take care of my father. If you guys need cash, why don't you help sell some of our delicious, mouth-watering samosas and get paid for it?"

"Sounds like a plan."

"Are you guys hungry? We have band-samosa, which is a poor man's food famous in Kasauli."

"We are starving and could do with some food."

"Wonderful! I will get some for you right away."

The next day, the children took the band-samosas to the nearby church and set up shop there. They had experience in buying and selling vegetables, so this was easy work.

They put up a sign board that read: "Jitender's Band-Samosas." Since Jitender was well-known in Kasauli, this was a good marketing idea.

By the time the sunlight had gone, they had sold over 500 Rs worth of samosas and was given a fifteen-percent commission for their efforts.

Kumar got a call from his mom.

"Darling, we will be home in another couple of hours after clearing customs and collecting our baggage. Hope to see you all soon."

Kumar gulped. "What are we going to do?"

"There is only one thing we can do. Call your mother and tell her that we are having dinner and will be a little late."

"Why do I feel that you have a plan, Ram?"

"Just do it, will ya?"

Kumar did what Ram told him.

The children thanked Jitender and left. Ram led them to the site of the crash. He took the "VICTORY IS OURS" banner.

Kumar understood. "Taking a page from the Egyptian tales, are we? The Alibaba story, if told in Indian-style, eh?"

"What is this 'eh' stuff?"

"I saw a Canadian movie—it influenced me a little."

"The wind is in my hair. It is getting cold. I wish that we had the chariot instead."

"I feel that the wind will dislodge us."

"Not if we go slow."

When they got home, they were tired. They welcomed their parents, who had checked to see if the chariot was there, and when it wasn't, they were sure that the idea of their children flying the chariot was nonsense.

Leela's parents were worried till Lakshmi came over to tell them that Leela was already asleep at his house.

That was a close call, Lakshmi thought to herself.

After the tired parents went to bed, the children congregated on the terrace.

"What are we going to do now?"

"We have to find Leela and the two backstabbers and teach them a lesson that they will not forget."

"How are we going to do that?"

"My phone is with Leela." Ram's eyes were glittering in the dark. "If my mother can trace me, then I can trace Leela too. And here it comes in this app. She is in...um...Sri Lanka."

"Sri Lanka? How many of our neighboring countries are we going to visit this week? I heard that the beaches there are amazing."

They set a course for Sri Lanka. Their makeshift magic carpet (which was, in fact, the "VICTORY IS OURS" banner) was all they needed.

"Look, that is the tip of India: Kanyakumari, and there is the world-famous Thiruvalluvar statue. Awesome. It's so tall."

After traveling the distance, they found the chariot on a secluded part of a beach.

"It is a beautiful, isolated beach. They have the book. Can you see them sitting inside trying to read the book of time?" Lakshmi whispered even though they were not in earshot.

"Where is Leela?" Ram was concentrating on saving his friend. The book was a lower priority for him.

"They have her tied up. She is placed against the coconut tree there. They have parked the chariot close to the tree."

Ram was running toward the chariot. Roger and Sheesha were busy with the book and did not notice till Ram's foot dislodged Roger's jaw. Sheesha screamed, but the anger in Ram did not subside.

"You will not hit a woman, will you, Ram?"

"Behave like a lady and get treated like one, but behave like vermin, and you get treated that way." Ram was about to hit her on the shoulders when Kumar stepped in.

"The world will not see your logic, Ram. In their eyes, you will be wrong, even though she committed a crime. I cannot watch people get the better of you. Let it go, man."

"Kumar, untie Leela. Let's find out how she is."

They saw an injury on Leela's head, but she seemed to come to her senses when she saw her friends. "You guys are here? How?"

"It's a long story. It is time we go back home."

"You do not understand what it is like to live with a drunkard father." Spit was flying all over the place from Roger's mouth as he wildly looked around for a place to escape. "I don't want to go back for your stupid friend. I want to fast-forward and go to the future. Leave us here if you want, but I am not going back to my father."

"Go to hell, man."

The children left with Leela.

"Are we going to Valluvar Kottam to park the chariot, or what?"

"We will take Leela home first, and then we can do the rest later."

Leela ate at Lakshmi's house and went to bed.

The next day, the parents paid the Pakistan hotel that they were staying in via online banking and requested that they mail the stuff to Chennai.

"Leela," cried her mother. "You are getting fatter by the second. You need to exercise."

"Yes, Mum."

The children met up on the terrace, which was their favorite spot.

"Shall we have a look at this book, then?"

The group poured for hours over the book.

"I can't make heads or tails of this book. We are no better than Roger at figuring this out. What are we going to do?"

In the meantime, the media had come rushing to their houses when they heard that the children were back from their expedition.

"If you don't go away, we will call the police, you pesky little mongrels."

"No need to call us names, you worthless oaf. Jonathan is your name, right? Where are your kids?"

"I am trying to figure that out for myself."

The kids got out of there. They flew to Besant Nagar beach to sit and contemplate.

"I like beaches. The soothing sound of the never-ceasing waves is soul-calming."

"Thanks for listening to your spirit."

"Why not? We are not physical beings. We should try to

learn spirituality."

"I got it," Rocky said.

"How?"

"Do you see the sunlight? Let it pass through the pages. The shadow that falls makes it readable."

"You are the best, Rocky."

"I already know that."

"So humble, aren't you?"

"Ha, ha, ha."

"Let's go back home."

They reached their place, only to find a huge rock had fallen through the roof. The children rushed in to see their folks lying unconscious.

"Call the emergency number for the ambulance," Ram commanded.

"On it." Ali was already dialing the number.

"Ram? Ram, where are you going?" Rocky asked.

That was when Leela saw another chariot in the air—a little smaller than theirs and more aerodynamic.

"Where did he get that chariot from?" Ali wondered. Then someone came online, and he started speaking to the emergency services.

"Looks like someone took it from Mahabalipuram." Leela paused. "No, he has taken a chariot from Sri Lanka and flew here."

"Ram, let it be. Don't race off after Roger. It is not worth it." Ram had taken their chariot and chased him.

"He messed up my roof. I will kill him." Ram was incredulous.

Lakshmi looked worried as she whispered to Leela, "He does not mean that, does he?"

"I don't know what he means sometimes." Leela looked worried. Roger must have found a way to fly here as well.

The children were peering up to see what was happening as Rocky gave the commentary:

"They are banging into each other. Ram's chariot is bigger, and so this must have affected Roger's chariot."

But no, the larger chariot was also older, and so cracks were showing on it.

"Ram is jumping into the smaller chariot. There goes the Valluvar Kottam chariot. I hope that it does not fall on anyone's head. That could be tragic."

"Right ray of sunshine, aren't you?"

On the craft, Roger punched Ram in his gut, and Ram folded to the ground.

The craft wobbled as both controlled it. It dove deep.

"Oh, God, the Valluvar Kottam chariot has fallen onto the road and is right in the heart of the traffic. That will raise eyebrows."

"Concentrate on Ram, here. Hello?"

"Ram is flying toward the river. Does Roger know how to swim? Because I am sure that Ram can swim."

"We need to help them. Looks like Roger cannot." Ram and Roger were trying to float and were spluttering water. The river's source was the sea, and the saltwater enabled them to float a little.

All the children rushed to the aid of Ram and Roger, who at this point were clinging on to each other for support.

The boat club nearby had lifeguards. The large men took to their boats immediately. They helped the boys and pulled them to safety. Both children were soaking wet, and the wind chilled them a little.

The children parted ways with Roger.

"Never come to visit us, ever."

"I don't want to. You guys were the worst. I hate all of you."

The crow that Ram had saved earlier flew in and took a dump on Roger.

"Ha, ha. You stink, Roger, and even my crow knows that."

"Get lost."

By this time, the medical team had helped the parents.

"Will the insurance company cover the costs?"

"I don't think that they will."

"Why not?"

"Boulders falling through the roof is not in the policy, now, is it?"

"Darn it."

"Time to save Gopal."

The children shopped in the evening to purchase a guard for Gopal's genitals so that he would not be in danger when he played against the opposing team in the future.

Then, the children traveled back in time.

"Hello, children. It is nice to meet you all again. I knew that you could do it." The old man was back.

"Isn't he the guy you were speaking to at the hospital? The guy who told you the story of these books?" Ali was gaping in surprise.

"Yes." Leela felt confused, and then she got angry. "If you knew the secret of how to go back in time, then you could have told us right away. We nearly died while trying to get the book. Did you know that?"

"But like I said: Only the worthy will find the book and translate it. All of you, if you like, are welcome to join the secret society."

"Just like that?"

"You have earned it. Obviously, Gopal will be the only one who will have the ability to read the book of the dead."

"Can you help us to revive Gopal?" Ram did not want to make any mistake. They were too close to the end to mess it up now.

"Don't worry, I have already spoken with him and changed the course of time. It will be like he never died."

Gopal was oblivious to the entire situation. The children hugged him, and Leela would not let go. She had tears pouring from her eyes.

Gopal came to know about Leela's pregnancy and was more thrilled than a kid with a gift in his hands.

"How are we going to explain this to our parents?" Gopal was biting his nails.

"I think we don't have to. We can go back in time and erase that part of our life until we are ready for it." Leela placed her hands on his chest. It felt good to do so.

The old man pointed at his own chariot, which was the Thiruvarur chariot—one of the tallest and largest chariots in the world.

"Whoa...you're taking that?" Ali was amazed and impressed.

"The place we are headed requires a more powerful chariot than the Valluvar Kottam chariot—that is, if you are interested in entering the secret society?" The wrinkles in the man's face became prominent as he smiled. "I am Ken," he introduced himself.

"We are interested," Gopal piped up. He felt left out of this adventure. *I'm going to take the lead in the next stage of this adventure,* he thought.

"Good, then hop on."

They flew way up into the sky.

"Why am I not feeling cold?"

"There is more to flying than just flying. You won't feel cold, nor will you be left breathless. There is plenty of oxygen here."

"Why are we still climbing? We have gone high enough. I am feeling dizzy already."

"We are leaving Earth, my dear boy."

"What? Why? Where are we going?"

"Into a black hole. Do you know what a black hole is?"

"It sucks everything into it, and not a single thing escapes it."

"True. Ever wonder where it disappears off to?"

"I don't know, and if I am right, no one else does either."

"Wrong. I know what is inside a black hole."

"You do?"

"Yes."

"Well, what is it?"

"Our universe is like a big balloon. What happens when you prick a balloon?"

"The air gushes out."

"Exactly! That happens here."

"There is a universe that is bigger than our universe?"

"Yes. There is so much more for you to see. Let your imagination run wild, and even then, you still won't believe what is out there."

"Okay. If nothing comes back from the black hole, how did you come back?"

"You forgot something: We are in an anti-gravitational craft. Even if the force of the gravity playing on the black hole is humongous, we will still be able to come out. Not a problem at all. Therefore, we have never been detected by anyone until now."

The End

Printed by Libri Plureos GmbH in Hamburg, Germany